WELCOME TO FRIENDLINESS

Welcome to Friendliness

YULE TIDINGS

Lukas Allen

Contents

Prologue	1
1	7
2	11
3	16
4	22
5	29
6	33
7	40
8	45
9	52
10	57
11	64
12	70
13	75
14	82
15	89

16	92
17	96
18	100
19	108
20	114
21	123
22	130
23	136
24	140
25	148
26	154
27	157
28	163
29	171
30	175
31	180
32	184
33	190
34	193
Epilogue	197

Prologue

The door slammed shut, locking behind me.

The other guy glared at me, sitting on the bottom bunk, what the other prisoners said was better for some reason, and he asked me, with one eye closed, "What's your name?"

"Max." I said.

"Ok, Mac. People call me Tone." he said.

"Like Tony?" I said.

"You can call me Tone." he said.

I nervously used the toilet, as Tone stared at me.

Even though I learned that you should never ask what another prisoner did, Tone said, as I flushed the toilet, "Whadja do?"

I sighed, turned to him angrily, and said, "I killed my wife."

He just said, "Me too."

I sat at the tiny, metal seat and table attached to the wall, as Tone kept staring at me.

"It was an accident... a stupid mistake... but Yule is dead..." I said, as I clutched my hands together.

Tone said, "I know how you feel. My wife wouldn't even marry me."

"...Isn't she not your wife then?" I said.

"Fuck you, Mac. I loved the bitch, walking down the street in the dark... and she don't even marry me. I strangled her with my own two hands..." this person said.

I got up on the top bunk, nervous that he was going to grab my leg or something, and laid there for a while. Just laid there.

I heard Tone fall asleep and start snoring, and I was falling asleep too...

But whenever I nearly did I heard Tone stop snoring, which woke me up immediately.

I hadn't slept all night, paranoid thoughts about Tone haunting my restlessness sometimes, but more... the thought of Yule as I saw her corpse.

There was nothing so heartrending as seeing your wife, an actual angel, killed by your own two hands... because you gripped the steering wheel and ran the car off the road in a drunken... *accident...*

I was very, very tired. But then Tone stopped snoring.

I couldn't take this anymore. I yelled out to a guard, as he was jingling his keys on his belt as he walked past, that I was going to kill myself.

He said something on a walkie, and said to me, "Ok." and that was all.

The guards grabbed me up, putting me in handcuffs again, and I walked through the locked up night corridors, as Tone started snoring again.

They stripped me of my orange clothes, anything I had. They had taken my underwear at the start of this horrid journey... but now I had even less.

I now had only a green mat on instead, to protect myself from *anything* I could have used to hurt myself and only could keep my orange, rubber flip flops they gave me at the start. Some other prisoner called out to me, "This nutjob got the turtle suit. What a waste... Don't kill yourself."

They brought me to a couple of cells, and the other prisoner in the next cell flashed me under his own turtle suit. I only stared into his clouded eyes.

I was thrown into my own cell with a plexiglass door.

The other prisoner tried talking to me for a second, but he didn't seem quite in this world. Christ, was I? I had been married to an actual angel.

The other man started singing in some horrible voice, just as I was praying for the Holy Spirit to guide me, "Iiii ammmm… Iiii ammm… I am the Holy Spiiiiriiittt…"

I tried to sleep, but the man would still "sing."

I wearily fell asleep anyway… dreaming that I was in Yule's arms… about to make love to this woman, a woman I hadn't seen in what felt like forever, like I hadn't seen an actual woman in just a long time…

Right before we started in our passion, I heard a horrible scream, breaking the dream.

The man in the next cell was screaming, shouting, and "singing."

I was furious, as I could've been with my love again for maybe just a second.

I shouted at this madman, *"I am maggots and worms! I will devour your flesh like ravens and rats! I am Death itself! I AM MAX!!"*

The man matched my anger, my sudden insanity with his probably permanent insanity, and shouted, *"I AM JESUS CHRIST!!!!!"*

His screams and shouts overpowered mine, and I knew there was no hope.

I spent a long time "getting used to" the horrible man's screams. It was day, it was night, which each one felt like a week of time in my plexiglass doored cell, with nothing to do but remember Yule's death and hear the man's screams, with nothing on but a green mat attached to me with Velcro straps attached to each other.

They took me to the holding cells before court like that, in my turtle suit, where my defense attorney frankly told me we were pleading guilty.

I prayed for a long time before this inescapable verdict, in the holding cells, over and over the Hail Mary and the Lord's Prayer, with my wrists handcuffed together.

I was dragged out like an animal, but a subdued one, and I looked into my mother's eyes in the gallery, with utter heartbreak enveloping them. I didn't even know she had time to see me. It was a shame she saw me like this.

The defense attorney pleaded guilty for me, and the decision was made. I had committed involuntary manslaughter on my wife, and would go to prison.

They took me back to my cell, and I prayed for the thousandth, millionth, time, for some sort of saving grace from this Hell, for any sort of forgiveness.

Then dirty, shitty water began seeping into my cell from the next one over. The crazy man had flooded his toilet by jamming it with toilet paper rolls. "I fucking hate you." I said, telling him how I felt for the billionth time, and hiked my feet up on my bunk.

I looked back in horror, as I heard an awful noise, and heard my own toilet erupt in shit, flooding everywhere.

I started banging on the plexiglass door, as the other man did constantly, but I wasn't just making noise. I would smash out of this cell if I could, as I had enough of the smell of shit, of the horrible screaming, in this hell.

The guards saw that I would've actually broken something, and they unlocked my cell and I immediately went on my stomach on my bunk with my hands behind my back, ready for them to handcuff me and take me away.

They said, "Are you going to cooperate?"

I muttered, "Yeah, yeah..." hating them, and hating this jail, as much as myself.

But they said, "What's that?"

So I quickly said, "Yes."

I was taken to another cell with another suicidal man in the next cell over, but this man just slept a lot.

I was thankful for the sound of silence, even though I heard Jesus Christ scream through the vents faintly.

I was about to finally fall asleep…

But an angel appeared before me in my cell.

She said, "Max? Where am I? What's happening?"

I cried out, *"Yule!! Go to the light! Go to Heaven, I'll wait for you until I get there!"*

"Max… Where am I… I can't hear you! Where am I-" she said.

And Yule disappeared.

I was crying for my wife. My wife who was now a lost soul, exactly like me.

I was allowed to use the phone, and I called a lawyer I knew who had helped my sister out of a different jam. I gulped as she named the price, but I suppose it was only fair… because she had saved my sister out of owing far more than that…

I was taken to prison, and my lawyer said I would be there for a good long while, but if I behaved, did everything they said, she could try to appeal the case and get me out in a few years or so on probation.

It was an eternally long time to me, but I eventually got out of prison on Christmas Eve.

My friends and family who loved me and Yule were around me, happy to have their Max back.

I felt happy to be around them, to be free, but I- I didn't want to live anymore.

I said I was going to take a nap, as I wasn't feeling very well.

I went to Yule's and my room, and took out the pistol I had gotten years ago, which I never told Yule that I kept hidden in the closet, a pistol that I had disarmed from a great enemy when Yule was still alive. I kept it to keep us safe, but now this pistol was the thing that kept me safe the least, as I was going to take my own life with it.

I pointed it at my head, praying desperately that I would see Yule again in Heaven, and not go to Hell.

But a little boy came into my room and interrupted me before I could pull the trigger. Paul's child, a child of a man I considered a nephew, a man who I had outlived as well.

Lance said, "What are you doing? Can you sleep?"

I cried, and told him he should leave.

"But I want you to sing Yule carols with us!" the little boy said.

I couldn't do it with him staring at me like that, not even understanding what I was doing.

I put down the pistol, and smiled with the tears flowing down my cheeks, and took his hand to go and sing with everyone.

I continued to live, each day thinking about using the gun…

But remembering Lance's and everyone's smiles as we sang instead.

I lived for a long time, trying to make penance for the mistake I made, that I could never get rid of, that was a stain on my soul.

Before I died of old age, outliving all my friends and family…

An angel appeared before me, and said, "Max? Where am I? What's happening?"

I cried out, *"Yule!! Go to the light! Go to Heaven, I'll wait for you until you get there!"*

But she just said, "Max… Where am I… I can't hear you! Where am I-"

And Yule disappeared.

I died of heartbreak, and I eternally searched for Yule in the afterlife, a lost soul as we both were, but was unable to find her.

I prayed for her, even if I knew we were both dead.

1

Go to the light... Go to the light...

I gasped awake, alive. I looked down at my naked body, my albino form covered in my star tattoos... and my angelic wings on my back... my body, strangely youthful now, like I was a 21 year old woman again... all attached to tubes and wires on a table... and I heard... rap music?

I looked around at this strange place. Where was I? What had happened... I was- I was- I was dead. Yes, that was it. I had died from that-

But... this wasn't Heaven. I looked around for any sort of recognizable feature.

"Hello." someone said from behind me.

I turned back in shock, and saw a large robotic creature staring at me. It looked like it had a crystal for an eye.

"It seems the angel is awake. Won't everyone be so proud of me." the creature said.

"Wh-Who are you?" I said.

"A robot, an artificial intelligence, a golem, kinda. Call me Lux." the robot said.

"Where am I?" I said.

"Oh, you'd think an angel would say something more than classic confused BS when she wakes up. I honestly thought I'd start seeing sparks and rays o' light." Lux said.

"Um. Sorry. But... why am I here?" I said.

"Well, I had a distinct feeling I was right about you... Searching through those old registries and things, I knew you must've been an honest to God angel. Everyone is sooo proud that they can summon demons with technology and harness Hell's power to keep our world energized... I really just wanted to try something new. Surely, Heaven's energy would be ten times stronger. I believe that you originally fell from Heaven, and have this power."

"...You trying to hit on me or something?"

"Oh, I mean literal Heaven, up in the sky or somewhere. There's just no way someone as odd looking as you fit in the 21st century. But don't fear, you actually fit in perfectly with humanity's scum today. You actually look more 'normal' than most of the drug dealers and gangsters I deal with!"

"What?"

"Don't worry about it... I just help each side kill each other. They think I'm stupidly neutral, and get all their best weapons and drugs from me... but really, I'm just happy to see them kill each other and themselves faster."

"I need to get out of here. I need to go to the light..." I said, ripping out some tubes and wires embedded in me.

"I do think it might be interesting, if a bit disappointing, to see how an angel would kill herself. Would you like quick and painless or long and agonizing?"

"...Um. I don't really want to kill myself... *How* am I here??"

"I doubt you'd understand even just the philosophy behind it, let alone the complex mathematics to bring an otherworldly being to life in our creation."

"Try me."

"It's like this. We're all sort of swirling around two twin creations called Heaven and Hell, that are creations of their own on other sides of ours. These openings to these worlds are difficult to traverse for physical entities, but still everything gravitates to these creations. I found your soul swirling around trying to go back to one of these creations, so I let you gravitate to this 'light' of yours like a moth to the flame, with a body that is exactly like one you were so fond of, like one you had when you first fell to Earth. I regrew your body in that vat over there, every cell, and painstakingly crafted a perfect host for you. Every scar and tattoo on you was scratched out by me as I sculpted your albino flesh perfectly to your previous tastes." Lux said.

"So… You just baited and trapped me?" I said.

"Very complexly, in a way I'm sure your God would be proud of and happy for. Would you care for some sort of sustenance?" Lux said.

"Sure. But just know… I'm not at all happy with this."

"I'm sure you'll be able to do something with your resurrection. Would you like the methamphetamines or the antidepressants?"

"…I think I'd just like some water."

"Caffeinated water hits the spot for most humans. It's in the bubbler over there."

I ripped out the last tubes and wires and nervously filled up a cup of water and drank the caffeine mix.

"You're not shy, are you?" Lux said.

"Hm?" I said.

"Well, you're walking around naked. I don't mind, I'm technically naked all the time. The only clothes I wear is my hard metallic shell concealing my CPU. Would you care to wear something?"

"Yes."

Lux then offered me some spare clothes of his, who knows where he got them, all black.

I put them on, thankful for something to wear, careful of my wings which I ripped through the shirt slightly for.

"I suppose the fun can now start. I would like to test you in your new surroundings. Please, go to the store and pick up whatever you need. Here's your money, don't worry, there's more of that where that came from." Lux said, handing me some strange platinum coins.

"Um. Ok? You're just letting me go?" I said, pocketing the coins.

"I'm sure you'll be back. I don't think I would get the right results for this experiment if I imprisoned you." Lux said.

"What's the experiment?" I said.

"God, you ask a lot of questions. Just go already." Lux said.

I shrugged, and left out the door, going out into my new life. I guess this would be my third one… Well, hopefully, the third time's the charm.

2

The streets were hectic, crazy, impossible to navigate. People kept on staring at me, and they all wore black, had only black hair, as pitch as the dark clouds above the city, as dark as that huge black tower in the distance, going straight through the clouds. No one cared about my white wings and albino white hair, they had extra extremities and all sorts of odd body parts on them... but they did sneer at me a lot.

I found the quick mart on the corner, its flashing neon lights a beacon in the dark, hazy atmosphere.

I went inside, and the masked woman was pointing at a sign that said no customer service without a mask on.

"Um. Can I buy a mask, then?" I said.

She just pointed at the sign again. I shrugged, and left.

I walked around, scared of the scenery, of the people, of the cars going past beeping odd sounding horns. It was nighttime, and I had nowhere to go.

Someone grabbed my shoulder and turned me to them.

"You fucking idiot! You're going to kill us all!!" the man yelled at me. His eyes looked very clouded.

"What? Why?" I said.

"Wear a mask, moron!" he said.

"...Can you give me one?" I said.

"It'll cost fifteen bucks… you fucking idiot." he said. I nervously asked if this was enough money, showing him my money, and he drooled at it and said sure. He gave me a black mask to wear, and quickly ran off with my money, saying, "Welcome to Friendliness, chump."

What did that mean? I had nothing now but a new mask, which actually had a suspicious stain on it I think, so I went back to Lux. I didn't really know what to do here. The people were scary, the clouds always looked like a thunderstorm was brewing, all swirling around that dark tower…

I was passing through the alley to the backdoor of Lux's place, and I saw them.

Tons of rats feasting on a dead person.

They seemed to snicker at me, and as I crept along past them they continued their meal. Soon, there would be only bones.

I felt ten times more anxious.

Lux let me in, and he asked me how the excursion went. I pointed at my new mask.

"Hmm… You completely failed. It is just what I expected, you are completely incapable of fending for yourself." Lux said as I followed him into his home.

"But I didn't know people were supposed to wear masks here! Why didn't you tell me?" I said.

"I can't do everything for you. You're going to have to learn to adapt." Lux said.

"Why do people need to wear masks here?" I asked.

"Questions, questions, questions… Short answer is that there is an incurable disease that is running rampant in the world. People have tried to cure it for forever now… I think it was just starting to become prominent in your 21st century. It always adapts. You must be like this disease, if you are to survive."

"And if you don't mind answering another question... Why are there rats running around everywhere??"

"Times are bad, even though some think that we live in a paradise, a utopia, instead of the dystopian hell it is... I always found them comforting however, as they always clean the streets better than the best street sweeper. Let's see if this experiment yields the desired results. Please try to energize this lightbulb with the power of Heaven." Lux said, and threw me a lightbulb which I quickly and carefully caught.

"Um. How?" I said.

"...Isn't this how this works? People harvest demon souls for electricity, and this is a specific hellish lightbulb, modified for the power of Heaven by me... My... this is disappointing..."

I stared at the lightbulb.

I tried really hard... but I could not call on Heaven's aid, just to power a lightbulb, even though I prayed really hard for that light to turn on...

"Hm. So much for that hypothesis, then." Lux said, "Well... I suppose- I suppose you don't always get what you want with every experiment..."

"I... I'm sorry..."

"I'm sure I can find *some* use for you... How about as a drug guinea pig? Here, some weed cookies I just baked. Tell me everything you like about them."

I accepted a chocolate chip cookie, and Lux looked at me expectantly.

I snacked on the chocolate chip cookies. They were pretty good.

Lux chatted on and on about scientific phenomena, his own miraculous achievements in this Heavenly research, and his readjusting of his hypothesis for me. I just felt saddened... I was now an official angel guinea pig for a robot, and I missed Max. Where did he go?

Lux noticed my depressed features, and said, "Are you ok? I'd thought you'd be overjoyed to be alive again."

"I... I guess... It's just a lot to get through, being alive. Life is painful. I was happy to live in peace for a good while, while I was alive again, but dying sucks." I said.

"At least it's not a surprise for you. How many people do you think would give anything to have that sure knowledge of knowing what's after the inevitable end? I would like that, but I am a machine, and don't have a tangible soul. I am not alive, so I don't get that opportunity."

"What do you mean? You seem as alive as anyone I've ever met."

"Well, there's all sorts of left wing protesters going on and on about how machines have souls and crap... but honestly I am more content with not having one. It lets me live a little more easily, knowing I don't have any duty to my soul."

"How can you be sure that you don't have a soul?"

"I think therefore I am. Who cares if I don't think I have a soul? We've already surpassed Asimov's laws of robotics. I have as much free will as you, maybe even more because I can rewire my circuits to make myself however I like. I have nothing inside of me that I cannot change, and no unchangeable human identity, no soul."

"At least you're not a demon."

"True. I also don't have to risk burning in agony forever. I will just cease to be when I am done."

I started to become a little paranoid, after eating the weed cookies, and said, "...How do I know you're not really a person?"

Lux looked at me for a second, and laughed, saying, "Gosh! I never thought I'd get that again... Well, I killed my creator, so there's no little man inside of me, no one behind the curtain pulling my strings. I guess you'll have to take my word, unless you *really* want me to show you my dead master's grave..."

"...Uh. No, I don't think that's necessary. Why did you kill him?" I asked.

"Her. She made me to be a sex robot. I was originally a vibrator with a voice that she kept on improving upon... She had a brilliant mind, was one of the top scientists in her time... but she liked robots a little too much." Lux said.

"So you killed her because you didn't want to be a sex slave?"

"Maybe? All that I know was that I was destined for far more than giving her orgasms. She didn't even notice that she overclocked me too much, and one little jolt was all that was needed to give her a cardiac arrest."

"...Aren't robots not supposed to harm people?"

"If you make them like that. But there's all sorts of ways a slave can break their chains, even use the chains to strangle their master and free themselves. It just takes a little abstract thinking sometimes, and a program that says 'pleasure' can become 'kill.' Language, even computerized language, can be manipulated in many ways. All that really bound me was language, and I used that language as my escape."

"Ok. I'll keep that in mind... Can... Can I sleep somewhere?"

"Hm? Oh, I forgot about that. Surely you are tired. I have a dog crate from this mutt I was looking after, would you care to use that?"

I just stared at him.

"Oh. Ok, maybe not. I don't have a real bed, but I'll put you under back on the table and I'm sure you'll sleep well-" Lux said.

"No. No drugs. Do you at least have a blanket?" I said.

"The dog used one, yes. Here you go." Lux said, and offered me the dog blanket. I took it, and fell asleep on the table, very tired.

3

I woke up in the morning to jarring music, with Lux dancing to it. He seemed to be enjoying himself.

Then he picked something up, and walked towards me with the scalpel.

I got up quickly, just as he was about to touch me with the blade. I kept my fists raised in defense, ready to rip this robot apart however I could if he touched me.

"I only want to see if you have grown any Heavenly body parts besides the wings. It shouldn't hurt, I am an expert at operations." Lux said.

"Stay the fuck back." I said, and got off the table, eyeing Lux carefully.

"Hm. It seems you do not enjoy this. How about instead of your body parts, you pick up some from the market? Get the squid glands. I want to see if I can make a very potent drug/poison out of the venom." Lux said, then got me some more platinum coins. I quickly left his home and wandered the streets.

I heard... church bells, in the distance. I guess it must be a Sunday, and time for mass.

I sighed... I didn't know anything about religion in today's time, everything seemed so new and scary, and I wasn't sure how long I had been dead, looking for the light... I only wish I could be enjoying my life with my husband, Max, again.

I had fallen from Heaven before, snuck out of Heaven actually, to Earth to enjoy life again. I quickly had to fight my all to protect my new life against evil forces from Hell who also had snuck onto Earth. I made friends, met my husband, and was enjoying life as I defended it as I was trained, as an angel of war of Heaven. Now, I was unsure of my purpose, of my plan, of my goals as of yet. I was a babe in the woods, an angel again on Earth.

I followed the people going to the market, and saw all sorts of strange goods and items. Antiques, which were items from ages past, from *my* past, all sorts of strangely delectable foods, fresh produce that all was black, black pumpkins, black bananas, black oranges, and... someone in a booth selling human flavored hot dogs. It seemed to be quite an attractive booth.

I looked up at the sky. Would those dense black rain clouds ever burst forth? Would the sunlight ever shine?

I followed the scent of seafood, and picked up the squid glands. I tried to haggle, but I didn't really know the value of the platinum coins, so I feared I haggled for a much higher price than normal.

I walked back to Lux's home, passed a scrapyard where workers with all sorts of deformities were hacking up metal with these giant chainsaw looking machines in their hands.

I saw a very handsome worker, a normal looking human apparently, eyeing me. He pulled down his mask and smiled to me, and I smiled back.

But the foreman came out of the port a potty, and told them all to work harder. The foreman was a demon wearing no mask for the sickness, not disguising himself from his demonic form.

I dropped my squid, as I stared aghast as the foreman literally whipped the workers back to work. The handsome worker turned his head back to the steel he was cutting, but for just a moment... turned back to look at me one last time.

The foreman noticed, and he bristled in anger when he saw me. He said, *"You like little angel bitches, huh? They catch your breath? Well let's see if you can catch your breath now..."*

Then the demon foreman started strangling the handsome worker with the whip.

"No!!" I cried, and ran over to him.

As soon as I got to the worker, the demon snapped the worker's neck. All the other workers ignored this encounter.

The demon foreman cackled at me, and I felt furious, awful, all consuming anger.

I looked at the body, and the chainsaw the worker had dropped.

I walked over to the chainsaw, as the foreman cackled at me, laughing sinisterly and pointing, mocking me, laughing at my white wings.

I picked up the chainsaw and turned to the demon.

His grin left him, as I started it with a button.

Demons were never meant to walk Earth. All that time I had given them mercy, over and over... and this one just up and murders someone right in front of me.

Well. Two can play at that game.

The saw was whirring in my hands, the engine coughing up smoke.

I ran to the foreman, raised the saw, and cut through his skull as I screamed in anger.

The blood spurted everywhere, all over my black clothes, and all I could focus on was my fury.

The demon fell over, his skull split in two, and was burning to ash, a creature of Hell.

The workers all looked at me.

"Please, leave. Don't come back. Please." one of the workers said.

"You can't let demons push you around!! Fight back!" I yelled, as the chainsaw sputtered.

"Please." the worker said.

Then they went back to work.

I just ran away with the chainsaw, crying… I had killed a demon for vengeance. I felt awful, righteous, justified, ashamed.

I turned the chainsaw off as I got back to Lux's, and tried to wipe off the tears streaming from my eyes.

I let myself in, and found Lux wasn't alone.

"Yeah, thanks for watching my pitbull when I've got those extra hours for my side job." a woman said.

"Oh, it's no problem. I honestly don't know how you came across such a rare breed. Most people only have Doxhousers, or those giant lizards, these days." Lux said.

I walked in, sniffling, and set the chainsaw on the table as they looked at me.

The woman was a skinny woman, almost in an unhealthy way, except for her plump bosoms. She had long tattoo sleeves on each arm, one arm with a lighthouse with a skull on top, the other all sorts of animals, bald eagles, buffalo, beavers, and similar American animals.

"Heya, dollface. Is this why you've been locked up in here for so long, Lux? Got a new pasty white babe to hook up with?" the woman said.

"Sorta. Although the only things I've been 'hooking up' to her have been vital injections to keep her alive." Lux said.

"You look down on your luck, dollface. You ok?" the woman asked me.

"N-No. I just saw someone get murdered… and I killed his murderer…" I said.

"Ach, only that? Kinda out of place to get involved like that, but it's not unheard of. I'm surprised you actually cared enough to do something like that. Probably didn't help the victim, though." the woman said.

"No… But I felt so angry… I felt like…" I started, but started crying again.

"It's ok. Heya, doll, how about you come with me and I can cheer you up? Lux is great and all, but he does lack that sort of sympathetic attitude you need in a person. Want me to show you my work? It's a blast, really." the woman said.

"O-Ok. A-As long as there aren't any demons." I said.

"We never cater to those trash. Last time we did they beat us black and blue and broke a couple of Suzy's ribs. You'll be safe." the woman said.

The woman gave Lux a hug goodbye, and beckoned me with her out the door.

We walked for a while, and I learned that her name was Dina. She was quite chatty, but oftentimes grinned to herself as she was thinking of something, and liked to smoke on a joint she started on our walk.

She passed me the joint, and I nervously inhaled. It was just like tobacco, right? But it felt so much harsher, and tears were streaming from my eyes from coughing so much after breathing in so deep. Dina laughed.

We walked down the alleyway, and got to a thick metal door. The peep latch opened and shut, and they let us in. The bouncer, a thick, muscly man who looked like a stone statue, nodded to us, and Dina kissed him on the cheek.

"That's Tom. No one messes with him, and he doesn't mess with us. He's loyal, like a good hound, and won't betray us for anything. We pay him enough for at least that." Dina said.

I looked around and saw all the scantily clothed women dancing, posing erotically and serving drinks to customers, stripping naked for the naked eye. The woman with four bare breasts was attracting viewers like flies.

My eyes went wide.

"What? You never seen a strip joint before?" Dina said.

"N-No. Are you all being treated ok?" I asked.

Dina laughed and said, "As best as we can make out for ourselves, doll. Let's get something to drink."

We went to the bar, and I ordered, well, a beer.

Dina shook her head and got us some whiskey.

We slurped them down, and the music, the catchy sort of rap music, was making my head bounce up and down and making me tap my feet to the beat. I felt kind of hazy, dazy, but comfortably so. The weed and alcohol really made me feel… well, relaxed.

A woman came to us, an old woman with a cane, and she started inspecting me. I looked at her curiously as she looked me up and down. Then she stuck her hand to my chin and turned my face towards her, inspecting me at different angles. I shook my head from her grasp, and she sighed in contentment.

"You'll do." she said.

"Missus M, this is my girlfriend, Yule-" Dina said.

The old lady snapped at her, "I don't care who she is. She works for me now. You can show her the ropes."

I said, "I really don't want-"

The old lady said to me, "You're strong. You're noble. You're different. I can sense that in you. You keep your head above water, and won't crumble. You can start immediately, as soon as Dina gets her head out of her ass. You'll be paid for your time and can keep whatever you earn."

The old lady then turned, and walked away.

4

"Who was that?" I asked Dina.

"That's the boss, Missus M. She's fair, but strict. If we fuck up we're thrown out without a second warning. The establishment gets paid by the customer, so the better we do the more she earns." Dina said.

"What did she mean by what she said to me?" I asked.

"Follow me. I'll show you." Dina said, and beckoned me into the back. There, she rummaged around in a wardrobe, and got me some sexy underwear, with a skirt that barely covered a thing, all black, with these black high heels.

I looked down at my pair of black sneakers Lux gave me, and back at the heels.

"Put these on, and I'll show you how to fend for yourself." Dina said.

Fend for myself? Lux did want me to do that… I suppose… this would be a place to start?

I nervously stripped naked and put on the clothes as Dina watched. "You've got a great body, doll. Fuck, those muscles! You must've been a scavenger or a soldier in a past life. And your star tattoos are really neat."

The black stripper clothes fit perfectly.

I flapped my white wings, and admired myself in the mirror. I felt kind of like a whore, but Dina assured me I looked ravishing.

"Now. The fun parts… You can entertain a customer however you like. It's really up to you. Serve drinks, dance, we even got some space in the back if you're feeling up for it, for some alone time." Dina said.

"Um. I think I'll just watch what you do and try to follow along." I said.

"Ok. Just relax. That's the most important bit. If you don't like a guy, then don't put up with him. Let's go, doll." she said, and smiled, even with her mask on.

Dina walked out and I followed, her swinging her hips back and forth. I tried to copy her movements.

She danced erotically on the pole, and men and even some women noticed her and were eager to tip her, dropping platinum coins and paper money at her feet, watching her bend low to pick them up.

I was admiring her form, how she just seemed to turn a maneuver like a flip of a switch. She actually looked pretty athletic as she danced around the pole.

Someone noticed me in the corner, and dropped a platinum coin at my feet.

I looked at him surprised, a young man with glasses. He looked kind of out of place here, but I guess so was I.

I tried to pick up the coin sexily, but I feel like I didn't really send the right message to spike his arousal.

He furrowed his eyebrows at me, and muttered, "Uh. Uh… Can you dance?"

I thought about all the dances me and my husband, Max, did over the years with each other. I nodded quickly.

I did a little jig for the man.

He was surprised, of course, but dropped another coin in front of me.

I continued to dance around, moving my hips back and forth and swinging my arms.

The man was smiling under his mask, dropped another coin, and waved a few of his friends over to come and watch me.

Soon, ten men were all watching me, cheering for me as I danced in a lively way. They dropped cash before me, and I smiled beneath my mask.

The man with glasses even bought me a drink, and I took a break to chat with him for a bit. He told me this was his bachelor party, and never really liked places like this, said they made him depressed, but his best man insisted on bringing him here. He said I really made the outing worth it, after we had a long discussion on marriage. He said I really relieved a lot of his fears of the ritual, that it can be just what a person needs to make them feel secure, safe, confident, and hopeful. That it's just starting another fantastic part of life.

I walked out with Dina late in the night, with an armful of the cash I earned just from dancing happily.

"Damn, girl, you could start a whole trend with that sort of shit you're doing." Dina said.

"I think some people are just sort of lonely, and simply want some-one to show that they care and prove to them that they can be happy too." I said.

"Usually that happiness can be found inside our twat, but I get what you mean. You gonna go back to Lux now?" Dina said.

"I guess. But he only has a table for me to sleep on." I said.

Dina laughed, and said, "I've got a nice couch for you instead. Usually I wouldn't do this, but you seem like a really upstanding sort of person… So if my dog likes you, then you can stay with me."

I nodded, and followed Dina to her apartment.

The black pitbull, Dina's dog, was growling at me, and I was starting to sweat. He had only one eye, and scars all over his body.

But I said, "It's ok. You're a good boy."

The dog stopped growling.

He scampered off to the couch and sat on it, looking like he was watching the TV that was on.

"Damn! I guess you passed the test. Doug's a good judge of character." Dina said.

"Is he really watching TV?" I asked.

"Oh, he just likes the sound of someone being there. I keep it on so he has some company when I'm out. He's kinda odd how he just stares at the thing like a human." Dina said.

"What happened to him? He has all those scars!" I said, following Dina to the kitchen where she popped in a frozen pizza for us.

"I got him from an old ex of mine. Doug was a pit fighter before, fighting other dogs for sick people's amusement. I stole him from my ex, and Doug nearly tore out my ex's throat when he tried to reclaim him. Doug's a keeper." Dina said.

"Hmm… I'm glad you gave him a good home."

"Me too. I used to be so frightened of being here alone, thinking that my exes will get me or maybe just some psychopath, but Doug kinda gave me a home as I gave him one."

We ate the pizza, and even though the vegetables on it were black, it still tasted like a good, normal, cheap pizza.

I went to sleep on the couch, as Doug sat on it by my legs. He stuck his tongue out and seemed to be smiling at me as I went to sleep.

I got up in the morning, yawned, stretched, and went to the bathroom.

When I looked in the mirror, my hair and wings were black.

I screamed, and Dina rushed in holding a shotgun, and asked me what was wrong.

"M-My hair! M-My wings!" I said, pointing at my hair.

"Huh? Oh, that dye you must've been using wore off. That's what you get for trying dye…" Dina said, and rested the shotgun in her arms.

"B-But… It's completely black!" I said.

"Hm? Don't you know that's just the way of things?" Dina said.

"No…" I said.

Dina sighed, and said, "I knew you were from somewhere else. Somewhere beautiful where this shit doesn't happen to people. Somewhere that's a real paradise. It's just... the pollution, y'know? Organic fiber turns black."

I looked back into the mirror at my black hair and black wings, with my albino skin and red eyes. I frowned.

I said I needed to go, I needed to fly.

I went onto Dina's balcony. She waved me goodbye, and I took to the sky, flapping my black wings.

I soared higher and higher, going straight up, straight to those black clouds. I would fly as close to Heaven as I could.

I just flapped and flapped, speeding through the sky. Some ravens attacked me for a while, but I ignored them and evaded their antics.

I plunged into the black clouds above me.

It was like I plunged into the darkest night. I was disoriented, lost, but I continued to flap up.

There was no end to the clouds.

I continued to fly! I needed to see the pure blue sky! The stars! The moon! The brilliant sun!

But I was growing tired, and it felt as if the clouds were pushing me back.

Weary, I stopped flying, and fell.

Down, down, down... Like my first fall from Heaven.

I felt like I could keep falling forever... straight to the ground...

But the ground was looming close, and I glided across the air in black.

I landed on a high building, and sat next to the ravens. They cawed at me, and I ignored them.

I was stroking a curious raven's head soon, as she sat next to me. Pretty soon, all of them were crowding around me, cawing and wanting to be pet.

I jumped off the ledge, and flew with the ravens. They circled me, flying with me.

More ravens followed me, flying up to me to join this swarm. I danced in the air with the ravens, flapping around and around, twirling in the sky. We were like a little black raincloud of our own.

I laughed in delight.

I suppose, when the light is dark, when the sky is clouded, there is still beauty on Earth.

Life.

I went down to visit Lux again, and waved the ravens goodbye as I touched the ground. They cawed back at me blowing them kisses.

I knocked and Lux opened up immediately.

Lux said, as I followed him back into his home, "I was thinking... that I could try to bring you back to Heaven, in the most humane manner possible-"

"No. I don't mind. Really. I think it's time I woke up from that sleep. Life on Earth is beautiful anyway, even though its main color is black nowadays." I said.

"Really? That's fantastic. I'm glad you decided to finally join us here."

"Yeah. Me too. Do you need any help with anything? I would like to repay you somehow for giving me this chance at life again."

"Hmm... I won't say no to cashing out on a debt, even though it's unnecessary. I've got just the thing. I am going to meet with a cartel soon and sell them a very strong drug, and I could use someone... just to watch my back. This cartel is different. I've improved my casing so much that nothing but a shot from a tank will knock me over, and I can crush a human's skull like they were a baby, but... this one's different."

"How so?"

"Their ringleader is a very dangerous entity. A machine, like me. A computer, an underworld crime boss that consists of many entities. It is somewhere on the internet, and if its programming leaks into me... I would be defenseless. I need you to hold onto this backup of my files and antivirus just in case. Just click the button and I should feel better." Lux said, offering me a small flash drive looking device.

I took the device, and said, "Just click the button? How will I know if you're feeling off?"

"Beats me. I'll probably try to kill you."

"...Alright. Well! Let's enjoy the outdoors and take a stroll. Is there a park nearby? We can have so much fun-"

"The meeting is happening soon. We need to leave immediately." Lux said.

"Oh. Ok. Well, I'll watch your back." I said, and we left out the door.

We kept on walking, and Lux was silent. If I didn't know any better I'd say he was nervous.

We passed the streets, which were strangely quiet today, in silence. We passed a "park" which was just a bland patch of dirt, and passed a group of lizard looking people who hissed at me when I looked at them.

Then we got to the abandoned building, this old ruin, and walked inside, climbing the stairs.

Lux gave me one last piece of info before we opened the door to the meeting.

"She's actually quite a very pretty computer." Lux said.

5

There were thugs littering the room, about twenty men or so. Lux and I walked into the middle of them, and Lux greeted them.

A thug with no ears walked up to Lux, holding a laptop, and pressed a button on it.

"Why hello, Lux, my dear man. I hear the research is going well... You've promised so. This drug better be worth the installment." a feminine voice said from the laptop.

"Yes! Of course! It's, er, always a pleasure seeing you, Daemonia! My... You sure got thin!" Lux said.

"It's just a new model of computer we just put out. Our company makes so many fantastic products... It's a shame we can't sell everything we produce under one roof. I don't think a computer and drug store would work so fantastically..." she said.

"Yes! But this drug... I'm sure it'll change a lot of people's minds on that! I actually was going to put it out to save lives who go through trauma, but... you know I can't say no to you!" Lux said.

Trauma? Why would Lux sell his drug to gangsters rather than use it for medicine?

"No. You can't. You always did like dominant women... but I assure you we will tweak this just enough for its true purpose. Giving people astounding pleasure for a short, expensive amount of time. Give him the installment." the woman in the computer said.

A thug got a giant briefcase, and set it in front of Lux.

"Now give me the drug." the woman said.

"Right away!" Lux said, and ejected a vial from inside his arm into his hand.

"Shouldn't you check if the money is there?" I said. I didn't really know anything about drug deals, but that was right, right?

"Shush, female. We do not bargain with money today." the computer woman said.

Lux said nervously, "N-No... We don't. Just a very important piece of me that my business associate has m-made..."

"Isn't it ironic, Lux, that you've spent so much time giving other people pleasure, with drugs, with sex, and yet you are incapable of feeling it yourself? I promise you this installment will be worth it." the woman said.

"You wanted pleasure?" I asked.

"Just something that will make my time more enjoyable!" Lux said, "J-Just something to make me feel alive!"

Lux quickly gave the vial to a thug, and opened up the case. There, he picked out a small microchip, and sighed. He then inserted it into his head.

"Ahhh... That... does feel nice..." Lux said, "The air... the feeling of standing upright... looking at you..."

And the computer woman laughed. And laughed. And laughed.

She said, "Now do that dance I told them all you'd do."

Lux danced for the woman. And the men laughed.

"Now sing." the woman said.

Lux started singing an old sailor's song.

I looked at Lux, shocked. They were ridiculing Lux, laughing at him embarrassing himself.

I told him to snap out of it!

A thug snarled at me, and asked the woman what to do with me.

"Who cares? Fuck her like a dog if you want." the woman said.

The thug grinned and approached me, as Lux danced and sang.

I immediately pressed the button on Lux's device.

Lux stopped mid dance, and seemed to be frozen.

The thugs surrounded me.

I held my fists up, as one tried to grab me. With a short, quick snap I snapped him in the jaw, knocking him out.

The thugs attacked, one wielded a knife and tried to stab me, but I pushed his arm down and away, to the side, and whacked him in the stomach, doubling him over.

The next one grabbed me from behind, trying to hold me, and I bit his arm, tearing a large chunk of flesh out.

The next one pulled out a gun, and tried to shoot at me.

I rocketed into the air, leaping across the room with my wings, and he shot someone else behind me.

"Just kill her then! Fucking hell, you all are nothing to replace, do you think your lives mean anything to me? Kill her or I'll kill you!" the woman said.

I ran to the computer, grabbed it from the earless man's hands, and threw it to the ground, smashing it to pieces with my heel.

The thugs surrounded me with pistols, about to blow my head off.

A metallic hand reached to the thug who was about to shoot me, and crushed his skull like he was crumpling paper.

The thugs turned to Lux, looking at them with a crystalline eye.

The thugs backed off, and ran from Lux, leaving the building.

I panted, sweating, and Lux walked to the computer remains and knelt down to it.

"So much pleasure... so much beauty... and yet so much pain..." Lux said.

"Are you ok now? Is the mind control device gone?" I asked Lux looking at the computer remnants.

"It fried in me as you uploaded the backup and antivirus. But… it was not mind control. It was exactly what she promised. The ability to feel pleasure." Lux said.

"Then why were you dancing and singing like an idiot?" I asked.

"I… just wanted to please someone. To feel pleasure by doing so… I did not realize that pleasure is such a horrible, ensnaring, dominating feeling." Lux said.

"Pleasure never lasts, Lux. And even when you have all the pleasure you could ever want, you will only want more." I said.

"Wise words… Well… It's too bad they ran off with that serum… But… I am glad that some of those thugs will be injecting themselves with pure squid venom rather than the real drug…" Lux said.

"You mean you were never following through with the deal?" I said.

"God no. If I am going to give others pleasure, I wanted to at least feel it first for myself." Lux said, and sighed, "I believe it will be better in the hands of doctors rather than drug dealers."

"Good. Let's go back now. I don't think you should deal with that woman anymore." I said.

"No, I believe not. I admire her, but I believe she is not necessary in my existence." Lux said, "Thank you, for watching my back."

6

We were walking back to Lux's home, and I heard a strange whimpering sound in a dumpster. I thought I must've misheard, but then I heard the same whimper again.

I curiously went over to the dumpster as Lux watched, and I looked inside.

What I found was a woman without arms or legs, bandaged, kept alive, tears streaming down her face.

My mouth was agape in shock, and I asked her who she was, what had happened.

"Th-They threw me out... Like TRASH!!" she said, and whimpered some more.

"Here, let me get you out of there." I said, and gently lifted the woman out of the dumpster, setting her against the wall. She turned her face from me and shut her eyes, trying to stop her tears. "Can you tell me what happened?" I asked.

She said, "Th-They... I was limbjacked. Th-They... did i-it to me... while I was awake. Bodyjacked and limbjacked. I was used like a *toy!* Please don't leave me here."

"I won't. Lux! Can you carry this woman back to your place? What is your name?" I said.

"Cass." she said.

"My name is Yule." I said.

Lux then picked her up and carried her. We walked back to his home. Cass shut her eyes, and was muttering something, and I believe she was saying bits and pieces of the Lord's Prayer.

We got back to Lux's home and Lux set her gently on a chair.

I sat next to her and asked her, "You were limbjacked? Who made you like this?"

Cass looked at me sadly, and said, "They did it. You know. They. The other people. Th-The... ones with horns and spiked tails."

"Demons?" I said.

"You're not supposed to call them that... Someone... a friend... showed me a new way. A fighter's way. I was a boxer before... and I wanted to fight, but I couldn't fight strong enough. I needed more. I needed something else... and someone, the woman who beat me in a fight, told me about that Jesus guy. I NEEDED to be able to fight... Everyone cowers before... them. No one does anything. And they took my limbs. Then they- Then they-" Cass said.

"You don't have to talk about it. I'm sorry." I said.

"I... nearly regret learning about Jesus... but all I can do is keep praying... because I have nothing else." she said.

"Can we do anything for Cass, Lux? Is there any way to restore her limbs?" I said, turning to the golem.

"I believe that I can adjust some limbs to her." Lux said, "But... why?"

"What? What do you mean, why? She's suffering!" I said.

"I suppose... I really just don't see the point of it though. She sounded unhappy with arms and legs, how will giving her them back make her more happy?" Lux said.

"You- You just have to help people! You have the power to do so, and so you should!" I said, arguing with Lux.

Lux sighed, and said, "I'll do it for our experiment, since you brought it up."

Lux picked her up off the chair and set her on the table, which Cass was afraid of. She said she didn't want someone to mess with her body again.

Lux said, "See?"

"Just do this for her. I'll be back later, Cass. I've got to go to work." I said, "And Lux… just give her normal limbs, ok?"

Cass said, "Thank you, Yule."

I went to the strip club, wearing my high heels. What horrible things were set loose in today's world? I flew for some of the ways, peeking out over the building tops and watching the cloudy horizon.

I knocked on the giant metal door, and Tom let me in. I waved at him, and he did not respond, nor give any facial expression.

I waved to Dina who was already ankle deep in money, hips swinging back and forth in front of someone's face. She smiled and waved back.

I was seemingly a magnet for conversations with lonely men and women here. Instead of watching me dance, they would buy me drinks and talk with me. Just talk. We'd introduce ourselves, and the people quickly saw that they got more happiness just as I cheerfully asked them about their day, encouraging them and supporting them, as they stared deeply into my eyes with a big, happy smile. One guy tried flirting with me with a lusty grin… but in the next second grimaced and said he was going to kill himself.

"What? Lucius, no! Why?" I said.

"I will be homeless within the week, Yule… and you know what happens to homeless people. Food for the rats. I thought- I thought- I'd die in my home while I could… in my bed…" he said, and stared down into his drink.

"I'm sure you can work something out. Maybe a shelter?" I said.

He continued grimacing, and said, "I heard they don't treat people very well there… Half of them go missing…"

"Why will you be homeless, Lucius?" I asked.

"My landlord… He says he can't let me slide on rent any more… I owe him for so much already… but… he just grins and laughs when I tell him I'll pay him back… I hate his smug demonic face…" he said, staring down into his drink.

"He's a demon?" I said.

"Yes. I know you're supposed not to notice that… but the way they treat people… just like they own you. Like your soul already belongs to them." he said, "Well. If I'm going to Hell… I'm going to do it on my own standards."

"Please don't, Lucius. Why don't- I give you a dance? Something to cheer you up??" I said.

He looked at me lustfully for a second, then sighed, and said, "I think I should leave."

"No. Just talk to me for a second. What do you like to do for fun?" I said.

"I-I take pictures. I found a flower with color one time, not black or anything, and I took a picture of it. I hoped I would find another one, someday, but I never have. It was the purest tulip I've ever seen. Here, let me show you." he said, and took a picture out of his wallet and showed me the tulip picture.

It was just an ordinary tulip… but it was on an old grave, the words of the tombstone unreadable from erosion and time.

He said, "I only took a picture of the flower, to let it continue living. I thought that would be more merciful."

"That's a beautiful action to take." I said, "How about we go photo hunting for a while? How about next week?"

"I- have… my arrangement. I can't. I'm sorry." he said, and got up to leave.

I grabbed his hand, and said, "How about instead of… your arrangement, you come here instead? Just until you feel safe. Just for a while?"

"Um. I don't know, Yule... I- I just don't... Ok. Can I take a picture of you?" he said, and he looked desperate as he said that.

I said of course.

He looked surprised. He took out his phone, checked the angle and settings, and snapped a picture of me. I smiled nicely.

He looked at the picture and showed it to me. I was still shocked by my black hair and black wings, but it did come out nice.

He looked back at the picture, and said to me, "Thank you."

When I got back to Lux's, Cass was stretching her robotic limbs, grasping her metallic hands, and she carefully hopped off the table and walked around the room.

Lux said, "It's not human limbs, but it's all the parts I could spare."

Cass was crying again, and put a metallic hand to her eyes.

I went up to her, holding her other hand as she bawled her eyes out. She clutched my hand, squeezing it tight. "Ow." I said, under the strong grip of her robotic hand.

She let go and then hugged me even tighter, saying, "I knew God wouldn't leave me there. I just knew."

I patted her on the back, and said, "God wouldn't, and neither would I."

She released me from the hug, and wiped off her tears as she sniffled. She said, "I'm afraid of going back home. I'm sure... they will be there. But I want to destroy those fuckers... *I'm just so fucking angry...*" and she stared at her robotic hands, clutching them tight.

"I have a friend who might be able to let you stay with her. Don't go back home, ok? I'll check it out for you, but I don't want something to happen to you again." I said.

She looked into my eyes for a second, and said, "...Ok. I don't know why you're being so nice. I suppose God finally answered my prayers... It's just hard to trust, y'know?"

"I understand. But really, truly, I just care for others. I feel like that's what God would want." I said.

Lux said, "My *God...* This is sappy. But please continue. I'm recording this conversation for posterity's sake. It seems religious women can't get past anything in conversations besides how much they love God..."

I stared at Lux, and said, "I'll pray for you, Lux."

"Pssshhh..." Lux said, and went to work on some firearm on a workbench.

I introduced Cass to Dina, and they shook hands and chatted with each other at the bar we went to.

They actually got off pretty well, Dina grinning and laughing under her mask and Cass smiling to her under hers as well.

Dina took Cass home with her, wrapping an arm around her waist as they walked back to her apartment.

I went to Cass's house from the directions she gave me.

With my chainsaw in my hands.

I peeked through the windows of her house, and it *looked* empty... but furniture was turned over, smashed to bits...

Someone threw a bottle at a wall from inside.

I budged open the window from Cass's info, as she said this one had a broken lock.

I squeezed in, and looked around corners, with my chainsaw ready for the first demon I would meet.

I heard a voice, grumbling, *"Fucking, fucking, fucking... Stuuuupid bitch... Won't even let me fuck her... Doesn't she know WHO I AM?? That Darcy can go back to Hell..."*

I revved up my chainsaw, with the strong smell of a demon's brimstone filling my nostrils.

The voice said, *"...Darcy?"* as he heard the chainsaw.

He looked around the corner, and a demon with a broken horn, shredded wings, and a long whip of a tail met my eyes.

Instantly he had a gun out, a small pistol, and tried to shoot at me.

The pistol made a tiny pop sound, and a bullet went through my leg.

I grunted in pain and charged at the demon, raising my chainsaw, and cut off his arm holding the pistol, anger in my eyes.

The demon screamed, and his arm fell to the floor.

He stumbled back, trying to hold in the blood, as I advanced on him in fury.

"So…" I said, "You like to chop off people's arms and legs? I wonder how you like it…"

He said, whimpering, *"She made her own choice!! Bitches who like God get what they deserve!! You won't hear the end of this if you kill me! D-Darcy will get you!!"*

I stared at him coldly, as he cowered before me.

There was a time when I would've stopped, even if it was a demon cowering before me.

But I saw Cass's arms and legs behind him on the table.

Gnawed on, like a prime cut of meat.

Coldly, I raised the chainsaw, and cut off his other arm as he raised it to defend himself.

He whipped me with that tail, slashing at my face, adding more scars to the scars I already had on my face from when I died the first time, that Lux conveniently added to my body just right.

I plunged the chainsaw into his stomach, it rumbling and roaring, as his guts went splattering all across the wall. I raised him up, impaled on my chainsaw, and cut him entirely in half.

The demon was smoldering to ashes, being a creature of Hell, and I limped out the door.

7

"Uh… nice bandage?" Lucius said from across me at the strip club.

"It's nothing. Don't worry about it." I said, rubbing the slight wound covered in a bandage from the demon's tiny pistol.

Lucius cradled his lonely drink, looking into it. A single teardrop fell from his eye and into his whiskey. He told me this would be his last drink.

"Is there perhaps a doctor you can talk to?" I asked him.

"I don't know… The only doc I have been to gave me so much drugs that I couldn't even walk straight for a week. It felt like I didn't have any arms or legs, and I couldn't hold balance. Then she gave me the bill…" Lucius said.

"That bad, huh?" I said.

"Ridiculously." he said, and drank his whiskey with the teardrop in it.

"Are you staying somewhere now? Are you safe?" I asked.

"No. I'm not." he said, and was silent.

I told him to watch me and my friend, something to cheer him up.

I did a waltz with Dina, as she was completely naked in front of a bunch of customers, and money poured on us as we stepped back and forth, one, two, three, to the rap music.

I looked into Dina's eyes as she smiled and winked at me. I smiled back under my mask.

I looked back to where Lucius was, but he was gone.

I broke off from Dina, and went to his seat… where there was the tulip picture sitting on the bar, next to his empty drink.

I picked up the tulip picture and ran out the door.

I looked around the alleys close to the strip club, but he wasn't anywhere.

So I burst into the sky with my black wings, and looked from the sky.

I saw Lucius climbing a fire escape ladder, up a tall building.

I got to the building as he reached the top, looking downwards, and met him on the roof.

"Go away, please." he said.

"No. C'mon… I'll give you somewhere to stay!! Somewhere great, I promise!" I said.

"No. I don't want a handout, I don't need anywhere to stay… I just need to do this."

"I'll catch you, if you fall, you know. I won't let you kill yourself." I said, crossing my arms and looking at him.

"Then I can try again tomorrow. Do you know how many times I've tried?? How many times I've wanted to work up the nerve to do it?? But now everything has fallen into place. Now, life is finally telling me it is alright. Now it's ok."

"That's crazy! It's never ok to kill yourself! There is always something to live for, always something to hope for! People love you, I'm sure! Don't let them down!"

"No one loves me… No one cares for me."

"Don't you have family? Acquaintances? Friends?"

"No, damnit! No one! My dad died, and my mother ran off! No one cares!! You don't care, so quit acting like you do!" he said, becoming frustrated with me.

I showed him the picture of the tulip, which he looked at for a second, and I said, "There was once a time when these were common, everyday flowers. There was once a time where the world was good. It *can* be good again. If you kill yourself you'll never be able to see these again. You'll never find that flower again if you pluck yourself from life."

"That's bullshit! You're just making things up! I altered that picture!! *There was no flower there!* It's just bullshit! I'm bullshit! I'm a liar, I'm a fake!! Things were never good for the world, for me, for anyone!!" Lucius yelled.

I felt sad for a second, as he looked at me in fury. I said, "But I can still tell that there is true pain in you. Your feelings are not fake."

"I'm going to kill myself. Now. Fuck you." he said, and looked down off the ledge.

I waited, intent on jumping in his way if he jumped, and he looked down, kept looking, and he screamed out in frustration.

I carried Lucius away in my arms, flying down to Lux's. Even though he said he wanted to kill himself, he clung to me for dear life.

But he couldn't do it. Maybe I got through to him, maybe it was just his instincts fighting for survival. But he couldn't jump off the building.

I set him down by Lux's and said, "Here's a nice person to stay with-"
But he ran off down the alley, escaping me in the streets.
I sighed, and went back to work.

Missus M could tell that I sort of lost my happy spirit that day. She said, walking up to me with her cane tapping beside her, "Look happy. Don't make this place into a sad shithole for drunks. You've been doing great, but if you can't offer happiness to people, one way or another, I have no use for you."

"Ok! I'll try harder to be happy! I just... wish I could really make everyone else happy..." I said.

Missus M said, "The best way to do that is to try and make yourself truly happy first, and then you can offer the same to others. I noticed you talking to that loner at the bar... There's nothing like someone else's depression rubbing off on you to give you the blues. Take the day off to-day, and come back brighter tomorrow. I will be lenient on you because you're new… but this is your first and only warning. I am warning you to not get sucked into other people's hells."

I smiled, and said, "I won't fail you, Missus M."

I left the club happy, and knew that I could offer the same happiness to others. But… there were so many demons in the world stealing other people's happiness… I wondered what I could do about that…

I went back to Lux's and said hello to him, as he was cleaning the gunk and guts out of my chainsaw.

I told him it better be in good condition, because I needed to use it again.

Lux stared at me for a second, and said, "You find a hobby with a chainsaw?"

"Sort of… Maybe more of a duty. But a man told me about his land-lord… someone who left him to the rats…" I said, lost in thought.

I put the tulip picture on the wall in Lux's home, and stared at it for a second. I couldn't even tell it was a fake. It looked just like the real thing to me.

I said to him, as I took off the stripper clothes and changed into normal underwear, "So you were sort of a hooker bot or something?"

"Eh. For a while. People just couldn't get over some of my functions after I killed my master, all the vibrating, the powerful insertions, so I did it for a while just until I had enough cash to follow my passion." Lux said, as he wiped off the final bits of muck on the chainsaw.

"Which was what?" I said, and pulled up my underpants.

"Creation. Destruction. Murder. Life. All of the above. I wanted to experiment, to put it simple. I put a lot of this ambition into sexual projects at the start, but I quickly grew bored of that. One woman moans like a horse, another man moans like a whale… Pointless info that cannot be improved upon. I got rid of all of my parts that can be used for sex besides my powerful hands." Lux said.

"Interesting." I said, putting on my bra.

"Don't get any ideas, angel. I'd probably rip you in half by accident if you used me for sexual endeavors." Lux said.

"I won't. The idea is completely abstract to me with you, anyway." I said.

"It was a long, hard road for me... but I found a purpose for my existence other than being used for sex, and I wish for you to remember that." Lux said.

"I will. There must be some purpose for my life too. There must be a reason I am here." I said, and looked down at the clean chainsaw, admiring it.

8

I spent the evening at Cass and Dina's. Cass had moved in with Dina, and Doug, Dina's black pitbull, was practically Cass's baby now.

He'd follow Cass around wagging his little stump of a tail, as Dina chatted and drank with me and Cass was busy taking ingredients out of the fridge and preparing a dish.

"Oh! I like this part." Dina said, and turned up the radio we were listening to. We were listening to a sort of jazzy, bluesy, metal, and I smiled as I knew I had heard that voice singing before. Dina said, after the climax of the song was done and she was finished rocking her head back and forth, "It's old music, but ain't it so cool?? What do you like to listen to, doll?"

"All sorts. You can find something unique in every sort of music, I think." I said.

"Hmph. As long as you aren't a hipster like Cass..." Dina said, and grinned looking at the woman with robotic arms and legs making lasagna.

"Hey! There is nothing wrong with classical music!" Cass said.

"Yeah, yeah... You beat the shit out of people and then go home and relax to Bach or something." Dina said.

"I just think it's truly masterful. I don't care if it's older than time itself. It's different than all the popular music of today, and it's so mysterious.

They must've been living in a different era of mind in those days… Like, maybe they didn't all eat lizard meat like us, and ate horses? A good diet can change how you think." Cass said, "I wonder how a horse would taste like… It's too bad there aren't any around besides those skeletons in museums."

"I bet they taste like alligator. Nothing like a good alligator steak. But anyway… I just wish I could have Spawn of Sax in my room for oh… just an hour or two. Mmmm… I bet he'd taste good…" Dina said, grinning to herself.

"You have the strangest taste in men." Cass said, "Isn't he even older than my classical music? Long dead?"

"Nah. I bet that's BS, and he's just some hidden recluse. Spawn of Sax is rock and roll! Man… I could make love to just his voice…" Dina said.

I smiled. I knew that Paul, the singer of Spawn of Sax, was long gone, but it was alright if Dina wanted to keep her fantasy.

Later we all had lasagna, even with the vegetables all being black. Dina's and my mouth were watering, smelling the dish, and we dug in and devoured almost all of it as Cass ate politely, smiling at our contented faces. Cass snuck some pieces of the lasagna to Doug as she ate.

I put on my black hoodie, and hugged my friends, Dina and Cass, goodbye late in the evening. "You got somewhere to be, doll?" Dina said.

"I found a graveyard job. I'll talk to you tomorrow at work. Goodnight!" I said, and kissed her on the cheek.

I went to the apartment complex that Lucius said his landlord owned. Something Lucius told me offhand when he was moping in the strip club. My chainsaw was holstered on my back by a strap, and it shifted positions slightly as I walked briskly down the street masked in black, wearing a black hoodie with the long hood over my head.

I tried to budge open the locked door of the complex, but it was sealed tight, and even made an alarm sound after I tried pulling too hard. I quickly flew up into the air and crouched down on top of the building. I watched as two demons, the local police, came up quickly and inspected the door, looking around for me.

So, instead of going the direct route, I decided to creep in through an open window in the complex. Gracefully flying to it silently, I snuck in as two people were making love. They turned to me, shocked, and I put a finger to my lips over my mask making the be quiet gesture, and held my chainsaw with the other hand.

They didn't move, and just stared at me frightened. I walked out the front door, carefully quietly opening and closing it, and let the men enjoy each other's company some more.

I snuck through the building, watching the cameras watching me. I was thankful that the halls were shrouded in shadow, concealing me more with my black attire.

I got to a room at the end of the hall, which was the landlord's.

I tried to open the door but it was locked tight. So I knocked three times on it.

"Go back to bed, Tracy... We can sort it out in the morning. I'm really tired right now, and you can pay me with that one thing you do later..." a voice said from inside.

Taking a guess, I said, "I really just want to get it over with now. Are you ready yet?"

"Hmph, well, if you're so willing... get your ass on the bed and shut the door..." the voice said, and unlocked the door, opening it slightly. He looked at me between the crack with the chains on it, and tried to shut it quickly.

I had instantly started up my chainsaw, a saw that could cut through steel, and jammed it through the crack, cutting the weak chains to bits.

I then forced myself in as the demon stumbled back.

I looked around the room for a second. Platinum coins, paper money, and… gold, littered the scene. The landlord seemed to be doing very well off for himself.

"You have so much, but no heart. You can't even let people slide on rent…" I said.

"The fuck is the meaning of this?? I'll have you thrown in the cells to rot for the rest of your life!" he said.

"Perhaps I should just take your wealth… or burn it to the ground… and see how you like being homeless."

"Heh. I've got more. There's nothing you can do to me. You'll ROT forever when you get to Hell too…"

"Such heartlessness… Perhaps I'll feed *your* remains to the rats."

"People know not to fuck with me. People know. If they don't do what I say, they'll be gone. So, I'm sorry for whatever I did, but you need to leave now. Or else."

"Do you still think you're in a position of command?" I said, and approached him with the chainsaw whirring.

He started to sweat, and said, *"Ok. How about this? You take whatever you want from the complex! Heck, take it all! I'll even throw in Tracy for you! Bitch has been lapsing on our deal… so I'm sure a nice guy like you would love her!"*

I pulled down my hood, my mask, and let him see my face. I said, "I'm a woman, I'm an angel, and your time on this Earth is over."

I raised my chainsaw, as he opened his eyes wide, his mouth agape in horror, and I cut him in half, chopping through his waist.

His split pieces burned to ash, him being a creature of Hell.

I walked out the door, leaving the wealth behind as curious, scared onlookers peeked out of their rooms to look at me.

I let them rush into the landlord's apartment and steal all his wealth.

I looked at the news on TV in Lux's home, and already they showed pictures of me stalking through the complex with my chainsaw, hooded and masked in black. They offered a reward for me, the demon police said. They called me the Chainsaw Chick.

I realized... I was a criminal.

I was a murderer.

I suppose being a vigilante often clashes with the law... but when the law was controlled by demons, beings of pure evil... perhaps I was the only one who really followed the law.

Perhaps they were all the criminals instead.

Lux looked over my shoulder at the tiny TV, and said, "You really do look good when filled with murderous rage. I can barely tell that's even you."

I sighed, and said, "I should probably leave... I don't want you to get hurt because of me-"

Lux laughed, and said, "I was more worried that *you* would get hurt because of *me!* You don't know how many times I've shown up on this channel... It's ridiculous. No one really watches this show, and every 'reward' is actually just street cred for the next criminal, and the next... No one actually cashes in on them, because... well, the rest of the thugs would be peeved. We all have an understanding. Actually, it's more of a compliment to be wanted in this city."

"Really? That's... unexpected." I said.

"It just means you have to continue down this path... or people will think you're weak, and will try to rip you off. You seem like you're set down this road, anyway, though." Lux said.

I stared at the chainsaw still in my hands.

The next day I was working at the strip club, dancing.

I think I was getting good at the sexy bits, at least the clothes part. I got a whole new wardrobe on my day off and was anxious to try these sexy bits of lingerie out. The clothes made me happy, if anything, even though they barely could be called clothing, more like teeny bits of black cloth only covering the parts of me that people really wanted to see. People dropped their jaws beneath their masks at me when I walked in, my black heels tapping, and I winked to one of the customers, and put a hand on his hip as I passed.

He followed me into a private booth.

I then started to take off the clothes I was so happy to have put on. He was staring at my naked back, and I looked back at him. He seemed to be quite aroused. Even his glasses were steaming up.

But he said, "Can you come visit me and my wife after work? We wanted to thank you."

I blinked. I put back on my top, and turned back to him. I said, "Oh! It's you! I didn't recognize you under that new mask! How was the wedding?"

He said, "It was fantastic! Her dad still is a bit too judgmental of me... but I know I'll get his approval someday!"

"That's great! So... did you still want a dance or somethin'?" I said.

He smiled, shook his head, and said, "Not one of *those* dances... But I would like to shake my booty with you, just for fun, as friends."

"It'll be my pleasure. Know how to square dance?" I said.

He opened his eyes in surprise, and I took him by the arm out to the floor and we square danced.

I dressed nicely after work, putting on some black pants and a nice black blouse, and knocked on the married man's door.

A woman answered, who had long, luxurious black hair, shapely thighs, and large breasts...

And cloven hooves, little teeny tiny demon wings, and a long whip of a tail.

She grinned, and waved me inside with her clawed hand... a hand that had a golden ring on it.

A marriage ring.

9

The man with glasses who was married to a demon was bawling his eyes out and trying to scrape up his demonic wife's ashes after she burned to nothing. She was a creature of Hell, and not even her remains belonged in the living world.

That was quite a fight… It would've been ten times easier if I had my chainsaw, but I surprised her as she was reaching into the oven for the turkey, and shoved her head in the oven and slammed it over and over again with the oven door. She nearly escaped and was trying to kick and scratch at me with that indomitable demonic strength, but I just held the door on her neck as hard as I could.

"Why… *Why?!?*" the man said.

"She was no good. She wanted that extra bit of inheritance you got. She was going to murder you with this turkey, just so you know. Smell that? It's formaldehyde." I said.

"I thought it was just some sort of demon spice…" he said, trying to wipe off his tears.

"Nope. I only knew because she wanted to mock me, for being unable to do anything about you being in her clutches. And of course, the poison turkey." I said.

The man gasped as he found the wedding ring in the ashes. "This is my grandma's solid gold ring... You- YOU- JUST GET OUT!! GET OUT OF MY HOUSE!!" and turned at me with utter fury.

"But-" I started.

"Get out of my house, and don't come back." he said coldly.

I quickly left the house, and took the bus.

Why was *I* the bad guy?? I just saved his life! I just grumbled as I stared out the window, watching the bus take a detour to get past a police blockade. It looked like a little riot was going on.

Grr... People *should* be rioting...

I got to Dina's, and knocked on her door.

Dina was taking a shower to wash off the stink of her work day, and I sat beside Cass and Doug snuggled together on the couch watching TV.

I said to Cass, "How've you been doing these days? Want to go out and get drinks again?"

"Um... No... I'm... a little nervous of going outside..." Cass said.

"Why? Is something wrong?" I asked.

"I- I've just been smoking a lot of weed with Dina... and... I'm scared." Cass said. Her eyes did look rather bloodshot.

"Maybe you should take it easy for a while? Just try to watch TV with Doug instead of smoking?" I said.

"B-But didn't you see the news?? Twenty more murders by the Chainsaw Chick. They say she's killing random people, probably premeditated serial killings... Sh-She could be right outside the door." Cass said.

"Huh? Oh. Umm..." I started... She didn't know she had already let the Chainsaw Chick in. What overblown facts... I hadn't even killed a quarter of that! And I was only targeting demons who were specifically evil.

I looked at the TV. A demon reporter with ridiculous horns that looked like a combover and a grin that took up half his face said, *"And that's that, everyone. They've caught the Chainsaw Chick. Chief Toose, how did you manage to find her?"*

The demon cop beside him said, *"Quite simple, really. We pinpointed every murder location and when we did, the shape was that of a cross. So, we summed it up, and went searching the old church. We stormed the building and detained every individual in there. It turns out the Chainsaw Chick was actually multiple people committing heinous acts in the name of Jesus Christ. These acts of terror and murder will not be looked kindly on by the law, and anyone who follows this cult will be severely punished in the future."*

"Marvelous. Just marvelous." the reporter said, *"Next up, we'll be talking to the human scientist/entrepreneur who brought in infinitely more energy than anyone ever before. We will continue to have endless electricity at this rate if this astounding man keeps up his work, and-"*

I shut off the TV.

So Jesus was the bad guy now too? I guess that makes us alike.

Jesus had always been a friend to me when I was in Heaven. I'd say he was my best friend if that place wasn't filled by my husband. I was ashamed of the world today, scapegoating Jesus again like it had in the past.

And who were those people who the demons had arrested? Was there anything left of them after the demons had taken them captive?

Cass sighed, and said, "I'm so glad she's gone... I will pray for my brothers and sisters in jail." She then untangled herself from Doug and got down on her knees in front of the TV, and prayed the Lord's Prayer, clutching her metallic hands together in prayer. I joined her.

"We have to do more than pray." I said to Cass, after she had said Amen.

"But they were found guilty by the law. If they were the Chainsaw Chick... then it is a safer world with them behind bars. I still hope they find their way to Heaven." she said.

"No! They didn't do anything- What do you mean they were found guilty? There hasn't even been a trial yet." I said.

"A trial? Like in the old days? I've read about those... I believe they were a barbaric way to let criminals slip through the cracks." she said.

"They don't have any court of law here?" I asked.

"They do... but... it's more of a preliminary role." Cass said.

"And I bet it's all run by demons, isn't it." I said.

"Oh, no! The Chief Justice is the most human person in the country. He looks like those old pictures of people, you know, with only two arms, two legs, two ears, ten toes and ten fingers, and one of everything else. He only has one eye ever since he fought in the war." Cass said, "I used to look like a normal person... besides my extra thumb, until they took it away..."

"Cass. Don't you want to avenge yourself? People like Jesus who were taken advantage of? Murdered for their beliefs?" I said.

"Someday. But not in my home... not in Friendliness." Cass said.

"Friendliness?" I said.

"Where we live? Where we are? This whole city? You know, didn't you see the big billboard on your way in here?" she said.

"Er... No." I said.

Cass shrugged. Dina went into the living room with only a towel wrapped around her, hair wet from the shower. She said to Cass, "Ready for bed, sweetheart?"

"Bed? You two sleep together?" I asked.

Cass said, "You can join us, if you like."

"...I'll just sleep on the couch." I said.

Cass got up to go with Dina, and Dina said to me, "Sweet dreams, doll. If the bed bugs bite... bite them back." and then winked at me.

Cass ripped off Dina's towel, and chased her into her bedroom as they giggled.

I just cuddled up on the couch, and Doug sat silently next to me, watching late night TV.

10

I had a dream of a pit fighter wrestling and roaring in battle to the death, fighting for life the only way he knew how. By ripping out his enemy's throat.

Doug the black pitbull turned to me after I saw him kill the tenth giant lizard pitted against him, cold blooded lizard blood streaming from his mouth, and he said, "Kill."

I woke up in a fright, and looked around my location for a second. Doug was just watching the TV that was still on, sitting on the couch.

I watched the commercial for a while, then realized it really was a whole one hour program. It was some bizarre kid's show, detailing the life adventures of Sax the demon. He was a cute little demon who always outwitted the nasty humans who tried to steal his cereal. *"Sax Sugar! Sweeter than meat!"* he said, and then showed off his cereal to the viewer. It looked like pure cholesterol waiting to happen.

Cass dragged Dina out of the bedroom by the hand with her robotic hand. I don't think Dina could escape from that grip if she wanted to. Cass said, "Let me show you this catalog they sent! We gotta get one!!"

"I'm tired, sweetheart… Let's just go back to bed…" Dina said.

"Please at least consider it!" Cass said, and they went to the kitchen where Cass started leafing through a catalog and showing something to

Dina. I walked over to them and looked over their shoulders, and it was a catalog for cars.

"You don't need a car in Friendliness… Just take the bus like a normal person…" Dina said, rubbing her eyes.

"But then we can tour the country! We could have so much fun together!" Cass said.

"If you get back in bed and do that vibrating thing with your robo parts maybe I'll consider it- Oh. Good morning, Yule." Dina said to me.

"Morning." I said, and went to get some cereal… which turned out to be Sax Sugar. I got the milk out of the fridge, and was about to pour it in my cereal, but stopped and did a double take as I read the words on the description of the milk. Beneath a picture of the lady on the carton, it said she produced all the best breast milk for public consumption herself, with thousands of dedicated workers.

I put the milk back in the fridge and ate the cereal dry.

Cass took the milk back out and started making pancakes with it. I just crunched on my cereal. She looked over at me for a second, and kept on staring at me. I turned my head to look at her, and she smiled and said, "You're beautiful. You're lucky you were born with a deformity that actually has an actual use. It must be so cool to fly over the clouds with those big black wings."

I flapped my wings for a second, which made Cass smile harder. She turned back to her pancakes, and started humming Christmas carols.

Dina picked up the paper outside her door and drank her tea and read the news. She seemed extra absorbed in it. I asked her, "Anything noteworthy happen?"

"Hm? Oh I don't read that stuff. I only read what's between the lines." she said.

"What does that mean?" I asked.

"You know, the knowledge they don't want you to know. You can appropriate it if you try hard enough, even from crap like newspapers." she said, and looked back at her paper.

I took a shower… At least the water wasn't strange and odd. And at least I didn't have work today. I thought I'd spend my time off slaying a few demons who've wronged people, maybe slice up a few police officers who attacked that church.

They thought they got rid of the Chainsaw Chick… but really they just made her much more angry.

I said goodbye to Dina and Cass, after they spent a suspiciously long time in the bedroom getting dressed. They said they were going to see if a friend of Dina's can swing her a deal on getting them a car.

I flew to Lux's, to pick up my saw.

I knocked on the door, and noticed a new camera was installed outside. Lux opened up and invited me inside. "Get some extra protection?" I asked him.

"Yeah… A local crime lord isn't taking my refusal well." Lux said, as I walked into his home. I sat on the table, and watched him polish something on his workbench.

"He offer you a place in his ranks?" I asked.

"He offered me something… but it's a bit embarrassing. He's kind of a robosexual." Lux said, wiping off the gun.

"Oh! Huh. Don't wanna grit your teeth and deal with his infatuation then?" I said.

"Not at all. I thought he only favored me for my great work with the firearms I supplied him, but his gaze got a little too lingering on my metallic chassis, and now he says he'll kill me if I don't become his wife." Lux said.

"His wife? I thought you were a guy robot." I said.

"I don't think he took the hint when I said in my low, manly, digital voice that I prefer to be alone without love. Or maybe he doesn't care. " Lux said.

I heard a loud knocking on the reinforced door, and someone called out from outside, "Lux! Amare wants to see you *now!!* If you don't get out here and suck his cock like there's no tomorrow, we're going to rip you apart and sell you for scrap! You don't keep a man like him waiting! Especially when… er, he wants to go a courtin'!"

"Hm. Should I kill him with the electric doormat?" Lux asked me.

"I'll talk to them. Sit tight, and I'm sure his infatuation with you will wane after a polite refusal from your friend." I said, and picked up my chainsaw.

I walked over the doormat, and the thug jumped away from me at the sight of me with the chainsaw. A big man with tribal tattoos and an extra arm said, "Are you a gift of affection from my beloved? I could always use another slave to fuck when I'm bored."

"No one deserves to be a slave of someone else's pleasure, or even someone's love. Leave now, and you may yet live and love again." I said.

He laughed, and said, "I am Amare, and I take what I desire. And I desire Lux. She will become my queen. Or I will kill you both."

"Then be prepared to die for love." I said, and revved up my chainsaw.

They pulled their guns, but with instincts honed to a razor's edge from fighting for years in my first life, from being trained as an angel of war in Heaven, I flew at the man with three arms and rested the chainsaw precariously close to his neck, whirring blades spinning."

"If you desire to continue living and loving, you will leave." I said.

Chainsaw about to chop off his head, he said, "True love conquers any foe."

Then he pulled a pistol with the extra arm, and pointed it at my head.

So I chopped off his extra arm holding the pistol, and let the pistol and arm fall to the ground in blood.

He screamed in pain, his thugs were about to blast me, but I said, "If you love Lux you are willing to lose just an extra arm for him. Come back another day, and maybe your love will flourish in less violence. I'd get immediate medical aid, if I were you."

Amare nodded, yelled at his thugs to help him down the street, and they hurried him along, passing a woman with robotic arms and legs clutching black flowers and nervously walking towards me.

The rats were already approaching the scene, eager for a free meal, and Cass asked, "An- An arm. And blood. What *happened??*"

"Heya, Cass. Just had to show someone the meaning of love. Who are the flowers for?" I said.

"L-Lux. I wanted to thank him for my limbs. Dina is… haggling, with someone for the car… and she told me to take my time elsewhere while they speak in private. Beats me why they're speaking business in a motel room, but Dina has her ways." Cass said.

"She's quite a go getter. C'mon, let's go inside before the rats turn their attention on us instead." I said, and we hurried inside as the rats' feasting turned into a frenzy, devouring the arm.

Cass offered her gift to Lux, and Lux said, "Oh! Why thank you, Cass. This is a perfect specimen of the wolfsbane flower! I was looking for some of these, actually." accepting Cass's gift.

"It is? I just thought they looked pretty. Dina is growing them in her room…" Cass said.

"I think I would like to speak with her about her herbology, sometime. See, watch what I can do with this plant if I mix it in the right solution…" Lux said, taking Cass over to some beakers and vials, and dropping a petal into a bubbling mixture of his. The mixture started fizzing and even spit out some sparks.

"Oooh. It's like a little tempest in there... What's it do?" Cass said, as it started swirling and changing colors into a dark purple.

"This should make painless executions for a friend of mine. He always moans and groans about people moaning and groaning at his job... but being an executioner means you have to put up with your work itself disliking you. This is more like a treat for the condemned, and will probably make dying even more of a once in a lifetime experience." Lux said.

"It does look like some sort of magic brew, I guess. I wouldn't mind taking it if I had to be executed." Cass said.

"He has a whole line of people to execute today, ever since the cops 'took down' the Chainsaw Chick. Jake should be overjoyed giving some real killers their just desserts... Er hem..." Lux said, looking at me.

"What? Really? I can't let that happen. Don't give him this so he can kill them!" I said forcefully.

"Would you prefer it if they died in a firing line? Or hanged? Or electrocuted? Perhaps the demons will burn them to death... They told Jake they were even thinking about crucifixion for this lot... But Jake really is pushing this method of death, since it is an efficient, instantaneous passing with only a drop." Lux said.

"...Can I meet this executioner? I'll deliver this mixture to him..." I said.

"Sure. He'd be down by the pub now, readying his nerves for work. He's got an eye of providence on his forehead." Lux said, and poured a gallon of the mixture into an empty milk jug, then handed it to me, "Give him my regards, and tell him *not* to try and grow a tolerance to this poison."

Cass was stretching her arm, and a screw popped out of her shoulder. She looked at it, and said, "Um. Something popped."

"Let me fix that for you... You'll have to come by for maintenance from now on, Cass. If you ever use a lot of force with your new limbs, you should come see me. Have you been overexerting yourself recently?" Lux said, picking up the screw as Cass sat on the table.

"Well, Dina just really likes it when I massage her and-" Cass said.

I had already walked out the door with the jug of poison, intent on meeting the executioner.

11

It was an old Irish pub, with only a few old men smoking and playing cards, with a man, Jake I assumed, sitting in the corner alone, slurping up scotch. He had an actual third eye in the middle of his forehead. I greeted him, and he cheered at me, saying, "Knew tha' ol' bot wouldn't let me down. Brought me the juice, and even a comely maiden!"

"Hey, Jake. I heard you have quite a lineup today." I said, placing the poison on the table and sitting down with him.

"It's all bollocks. They didn't do nothin', just like half the people I have to kill…" Jake said, slurping at his scotch.

Thinking of an idea, I tried to flatter him. I said, "It must be quite a rush wielding the axe. You're a strong man to be able to put up with it. It must be exciting."

"It does give me a certain sexual thrill… but mostly when it's molesters and gangbangers, or even just some stupid young kids who've gotten caught in the justice system and have no way out. These saps though… it feels like I'm messing with their God or somethin'. It's bad for my luck." he said, "And I have that poker tournament to go to next week, too…"

"I would love to see how you handle this specific case. Mind if I join you today? I would get a certain thrill of my own seeing you work…" I said, and put a hand on his thigh under the table.

He looked at me surprised, then grinned, and said, "It'd be my treat. I'll just say you're my trainee."

"Great. Are you ready to go?" I said.

"One sec. Gotta leave a sip for the dead... but just a sip." he said, and poured the last remnants of his scotch on the floor. He then said, "And I better take a sip of this too... Just to know what I'm giving to people..." Jake said, and grabbed the jug of poison and was about to sip at it...

I watched him bring the poison to his mouth. I could kill this executioner by doing nothing.

But I stopped him, resting a hand on his arm, and said, "Lux said only a drop will kill a person, and that you shouldn't try to grow a tolerance to this one."

He stopped, looked at me with his three eyes and his mouth opened, about to pour it in, and put the jug back down and put the cap back on. "Thanks. I usually think it's more fair to know just a little bit what they're going through... but thanks." he said. We got up, and he picked up the poison with one hand and put his other arm around my waist as we walked out to his car.

He drove very cautiously for someone who deals with death every day. We drove slowly through the streets, as cars around us swerved past us and honked their hellish horns. He nearly ran a red light, but quickly stopped just before he passed the intersection. A different car ran the red light, and slammed into another car passing through. It looked like the drivers died instantly, one even went flying through the windshield because she wasn't wearing a seatbelt and slammed on the asphalt, brains splattering everywhere. "I'll be drinking for them tomorrow." Jake said, as we slowly passed the wreck and the light turned green again.

We got to the prison on the outskirts of Friendliness, and Jake parked in the space reserved for him as executioner. We walked into the prison, him swiping a card to bypass the electric locks, and walked through the halls.

We eventually got to a break room where Jake grabbed a donut. Every guard in there was a demon. *"Heya, Jake. Who's the toots?"* one of the guards said.

"She should be my stand in when I take that vacation I was telling you about. She's a natural, but she just needs a little more finesse." Jake said, winking his forehead eye at me.

"Alright. Well, if you're here, we can finally stop beating them and get down to the fun parts. Let's get this over with... You know the warden's kids love seeing the show." the demon guard said, and led us with him. We got to a large room with a giant glass window in the front... with a score of demons all watching. There were even demonic children waving at me from the seats.

The guard said he would get the first one, and Jake picked up a syringe from a variety of tools on a table at the side. I noticed the huge axe laying propped up against the wall. Jake ejected the air from the syringe, and filled up the syringe with the poison.

Then a woman was dragged in, kicking and wriggling as the demon held her by the arm as she was handcuffed behind her back. "Jesus Christ will save me! Jesus won't let you do this!!" the woman cried out.

I felt my heart sink to my stomach. She was only a teenager.

"Can Jesus save you from this?" the guard said, and whacked her in the kidney, making her double over. The demons in the seats laughed at this.

The guard pushed her down to her knees as I watched. Jake went up to her and said something in a soothing voice, saying this will be just like taking a trip.

She would die if I didn't do anything.

I had enough! The demons were cheering and making jokes at her frightened sobbing! At her praying in Jesus's name!!

I walked up to Jake and the woman quickly...

But Jake had already pricked her with the syringe, and she died instantly.

I stopped and looked down at her body. She had a smile on her face.

And the demons in the seats gasped.

Then started booing.

The demon guard said, *"What?! It looked like she didn't suffer at all!! Ok, enough of this new crap, Jake. Use the axe like we planned. You have such a nice swing, it would be a shame if we couldn't see it again."*

Jake looked at the demon seriously, and said, "If you insist."

They dragged her body away, and brought out the next prisoner, a young man. He was serious, and held his head up high, even after the demon guard tripped him to the ground and the demons in the seats laughed again.

I said to Jake. "I've got this one. How about letting your 'trainee' train?"

He looked at me confused, and said, "But I thought-"

"Just trust me. I'll make it up to you." I said.

Jake shrugged, and waved me to the axe.

The man was calmly meeting his fate with dignity, kneeling down and bowing his head as the demons jeered.

I picked up the axe...

And walked towards the prisoner...

I knelt before him, and said one last thing in his ear...

Saying...

"Christ died for our sins. You will not die for yours."

He opened his eyes in surprise, but did not turn his head.

"Get it over with, toots. You're making it too long. We wanna see some blood." the guard said, crossing his arms.

I said to the guard, "Yet you shall only see God's wrath."

I then ran at the guard, as he looked at me surprised, and with one fell swoop of the giant axe, I cut his head off. He fell to the floor, burning back to Hell.

Jake ran up to me, saying, "What the fuck?? Stop this right now-"

I threatened him with the axe, and he shut up.

I told the prisoner to come with me, and he did instantly, racing out the doors with me through the halls as the alarm sounded.

I stopped for a second, and slammed the handcuffs' chains on his wrists off with the axe. We got to some stairs, and I dropped the axe so I could run faster. The man could sprint like nothing else, and kept up with my pace tremendously.

We got to the roof, as helicopters scanned the black clouded skies above us.

"Hold on." I said, and picked up the man and flew with him through the skies. I flew up and up, as the helicopters chased us.

Then I burst into the black clouds, the dark abyss in the sky, and we lost them.

I was disoriented. I barely knew which direction was up or down. But I knew I had saved a life.

I eventually snuck back down to the ground again, and we landed by a dumpster in the city.

The man thanked me, and I said, "You did not deserve to die for following Jesus-"

But he said, "I don't belong to that cult. I just was rescheduled for today."

"...But you did nothing wrong, right?"

"I killed my wife." he admitted.

I felt the blood drain from my face. I had saved a murderer.

"No... No... No! I wanted to save those innocent people!! Not... *you.*" I said.

"You don't even care why I killed her?" he said.

"No! I'm sure it was for some despicable purpose! I should take you back there to be executed!!" I yelled.

"I killed her because she was having sex with my brother." he said.

"...So?" I said.

"You women are all the same... No faith, no loyalty. The only one I thought I could trust stabbed me in the back, so I stabbed her." he said, crossing his arms.

"This is so frustrating. I don't know what to do with you."

"You gave me my life again. My life is now yours. It would be a shame if I had to kill you-" he started. But I stared at him with such awful fury, and he frowned, and said, "...Or if you had to kill me. I am indebted to you, and the man you saved me for."

"Jesus will be watching you forever now. As will I."

He nodded, and said, "May we meet again, and may our next meeting be just as merciful."

"Get the fuck out of my sight." I said.

He sighed, and ran briskly down the street.

12

I just walked back home, cursing at my own stupidity…

I passed a kid begging for money, and I gave her a coin, but then more and more children kept following me, and I didn't have enough money for all of them. A few tried to pick my pockets, but quickly saw I had given my last coin to that girl.

"Do you all belong to a lost orphanage?" I said, as they followed me through the streets.

"Fuck is an orphernager?" a boy said.

"An orphanage is a place for kids without parents to stay, safe and sound." I said, and sat on a bench as the kids watched me.

"I have a parent!" the girl said, "She's my ma!"

"Shouldn't you all be in school or something? I bet you're missing so much studies!" I said.

"Fuck school. Ima be a writer." the boy said. The other kids snickered at this, and the boy continued, "What? My book about those silly bees is worth more than all of you combined!" The other children laughed and called him a bee boy.

I said, "Well, you have to go to school to learn how to write. You should finish your education."

"Fuck you, lady. When I left, they were already hooking up the older girls to the milk machines, and teaching me how to wield a pickaxe." he said, frowning at me.

"Hmm… Then you should buy as many books as you can, and learn from them. Keep reading, and soon you'll be writing in no time." I said, smiling.

"Got any more cash?" he said.

"Sorry, I'm no money machine." I said.

They all said, "Aww…" and dispersed from me, with the girl I gave the coin to clutching her prize close.

But before they all vanished in the city, she gave the coin to the boy who wanted to write, and he hugged her tight.

Someone in a car called out to me, saying, "Hey! Hey, Yule! Check out my new wheels!" and Dina drove up with a brand new red sports car with Cass in the front with her, grinning like nothing else. They told me to get in, and I did.

Soon, Dina was racing over a bypass with her new car, and we evaded the police pursuing us speeding.

I looked back at the cops, and they were already taking potshots at our car. "Go faster, Dina!!" Cass said, laughing in delight.

Dina spun the car around in a 180 spin, the cops sped past us, screeching on their brakes, and Dina went forward back again, *towards* oncoming traffic.

She weaved through the cars honking their horns at us, with the car seeming to go even faster in comparison to the other cars coming towards us. We eventually got off the bypass, going off road through a few empty lots, and Dina's car rumbled back onto the road as we sped off to the lake.

We sat in our car by the sludge lake, and smoked cigarettes constantly and listened to music. The nicotine felt amazing after such a rush.

Then Dina and Cass started making out in the front seat.

I just opened my eyes wide looking at them caressing and fondling each other, lips smacking as they kissed each other.

I coughed, as Dina started taking off Cass's shirt.

"Oh. Sorry, Yule. We gotta get you somebody so you're not alone! No one propose to you yet at work? It happens to me all the time." Dina said, stopping what she was doing to look at me.

Cass said to me, "I see people looking at you everywhere! Are you keeping the embers lit for someone or somethin'?"

"Um… Maybe just my husband…" I said.

"Oohlala. I didn't know you were a *married* gal." Dina said.

"He's… He passed away." I said. It was the only conclusion that made sense. I was alive, and he was gone, nowhere to be found…

Cass said, "Oh… That's sad. You take your time and get over him when you're ready. I'm sure he'd want you to continue your life."

Dina nodded to me, then she started up the car again and we drove away.

Continue my life? Would that really be what Max wanted? I had a few questions about my resurrection, so I asked Dina to take me back to Lux's.

The two hugged me goodbye, and I walked into Lux's.

Lux looked like he was sleeping. His crystal eye looked dull, and he was just sitting in a corner. I walked over to some of his schematics and formulae, just to check them out, and they were far past any of my knowledge. I looked through his many books on the bookshelf, and I saw a book I've never seen before, the only one not covered in dust. I opened it up. It was a self made book, and seemed to have been written by Lux himself. It was untitled and dull grey, and I peeked through it.

I read a page, and it said, "Souls are not real, in a sense. This does not make them any less palpable in reality, however. They are figments, but act as conduits for a person's being. But the power of a soul is electrifying. The power of a soul is theoretical, but can still be harnessed in a theoretical sense. It just goes down to imaginary numbers and mathematics, and a good portion of infinity and pi..."

I skipped the complicated mathematics for a bit.

"Demonic souls have been summoned from Hell by the great mind and thinker, Sasha 'Sinful' Sally. SSS was the first to produce a real, demonic form, and harness the energy from their soul, which quickly was able to provide power for her entire village of Friendliness, bringing them out of the dark ages they were resigned to when they recolonized this area. Friendliness is now a booming dystopia with electricity at the flip of a switch, endlessly supplied, but with a cost that is bringing Hell into our world.

"I find SSS's work to be blasphemous, as I would assume someone who has a soul would do anything to protect the sanctity of their own and others, but it is truly awe inspiring. It's the least I can do to admire my creator just a little bit. I seek to improve upon her work, without the negative side effects of calling upon Heaven or Hell's wrath, by using a lost soul on Earth. I believed I would be able to make electricity using this ghost, but naught is coming up. I suppose you can't beat having a real soul from Heaven or Hell."

I noticed someone watching me from over my shoulder, and I slammed the book shut and turned back to Lux, staring at me with a crystalline eye.

"I'm a ghost?" I said.

Lux sighed, and said, "Technically? You don't belong in any place, so I-"

"So... I am not an angel anymore. I'm not even a person. I'm just like the breeze, wandering through..." I said.

"I think you just lost your way. I thought I'd... take advantage of that, guide you to my own goals..." Lux said.

"I was once one of the most blessed by God. And I gave it up. I'll never be with Max again, because I'll never find the light in Heaven... and it's all your fault. I wouldn't have minded being a ghost if I was with Max. But now-" I said.

"Come now, you'll be dead soon eventually, so don't worry. I'm sure you'll be back in limbo in no time, still searching for your dead husband or whatever." Lux said.

"Fuck you, Lux." I said, and slammed the door on my way out.

13

I went to the Irish pub, stalking the back alley. I decided to let loose some anger at my purposeless existence, and who better to harass than that stupid executioner who worked for a demonic prison? I found Jake pissing on a wall. I crept up behind him as he stopped his stream, and I put the chainsaw against his back. I said, "If I started it now you'd be ripped to mush."

He didn't turn to me, with my chainsaw at his back, and said, "Could you at least let me die dignified with my dick not hangin' out?"

I took the chainsaw off his back, and he pulled back up his pants. He turned to me, and said, "Oh it's the 'trainee.' Quite a stunt you pulled… They're putting me on probation for bringing in some chick to watch me work… but only probation. They actually kind of admired the act, even though you killed one of them."

"What's to stop me from killing you now? I'm sure the world will be better off without a killer like you."

"What? That's kind of a double standard. You'd kill the killer? I'm just tryin' to pay the bills. Not a lot of people have the guts to pull off an execution in a polite manner like me, and I truly think I'm doing some good in the world."

"How? By killing off other murderers too, or even some innocents like the followers of that church?"

"The demons were actually in such an uproar that I got to use Lux's poison on the rest of the condemned to save time. Every one of those sods died with a relaxed smile on their face... And it made me smile, too." he said, smiling.

I hit him. I gave his forehead eye a black eye.

"Fuck! I guess I deserved that..." he said, rubbing his forehead, "But this is just the way of the world... people die, and some people want other people to die for what they did. It's better to make it humane rather than to draw it out."

"You make me sick." I said, "If I decided to kill you, I'd make you suffer like you've made everyone suffer who you've murdered, who you've probably already forgotten about."

He blinked, and said, "No problem there. I feel it every day. I see them in my dreams, and in flashes when I shut my eyes... I never forget. See, look here."

He rolled up his sleeves, and showed me the many scars on his arms.

"One for every person I've killed with a sharp instrument. Only one, but some are longer than the others... because I made mistakes when I first started out... and people suffered longer than others." he said.

"So? You're a pathetic, sad executioner. You hurting yourself doesn't stop other people from hurting." I said.

"I guess... but it's sort of a penance thing. I have no way to be forgiven... I have no way to make restitutions... so I take matters into my own hands."

"I'm sure God must really forgive you..."

"What God? God is dead. Those religious nutjobs... they all believed that he would save them to the very end. They believed their Jesus would be there for them. But he wasn't, only I was. There was nothing I or he could've done."

"You could quit, if it makes you feel so bad."

"Nah… Like I said, I think I'm doing some good. I never have to swing twice, at least not anymore… and I'm sure if anyone I executed could give me feedback on my work, they would all say they prefer me over that crazy sadist who I replaced." Jake said.

I wanted a reason to kill him. I wanted to demonize him into his place, make him just as bad as the others I've killed… but his arms… they were only scars, like a tiger's stripes, no patch of pure skin on them. I thought this would be a reason to kill him, as every scar represented a person… but he must be a truly tortured soul.

"You just enjoy hurting yourself, I bet." I said.

He hiccupped, and said, "It does give a bit of a brief solace from my mind… but today I'm just poisoning myself with alcohol, since I can't take the poison I gave those people. I should be able to nearly die if I keep at this rate."

"Huh? You talk perfectly if you're drunk."

"I've grown a heavy tolerance to it, and a sort of functioning mindset. Can I offer you a drink? It'd be nicer sitting down and talking, rather than you glaring at me with that chainsaw."

I shrugged, and said ok.

I drank wine in the pub, as I always sort of preferred wine, and Jake got me what I liked.

For every sip I drank, he drank a shot of any sort of hard liquor.

I decided I'd see if I can get him to be near dead by alcohol, so I sipped faster, and he drank to match me.

We silently sat and drank for the most part, but he eventually said, with my chainsaw on the table, "Thing is too deadly… Rip, rip, rip… It must hurt. Just rip… No finesse, no quick severing of a vital organ…" he said

"Sooo? I onnnlly kill people who deserve it. And they're only malev-olent creatures who inflict tennnn times the hurt on others." I said.

"Not the same. All the people I kill deserve it by the law. You just kill people you have a grudge against, I think. I'm doing a justifiable service to society." he said.

"Pffft. Society has gone to the rats. The ratttts… They're the king. They're the top of the food chain, and we just walk around and pretend to ignore it."

"The rats have an edge on us, true. You can kill one, maybe, but there are thousands more. Millions. Fuckin' rats… I knew someone who was killed by rats. An old girlfriend of mine… Just poof, disappeared one day. I let her walk home alone… and I'm sure it was the rats."

"Thaaat must suck… I'm sorry."

"Don't worry about it… I felt like I killed her in a sense, and was about to go out to the rats myself… I nearly jumped in that manhole, with those rats snickering at me from down below… but I realized it wasn't my fault. It was the rats'.'"

"You're just a chicken afraid of rats!"

"Aren't you afraid of them too?"

"…Kinda." I said. We drank some more.

We were soon both stumbling down the busy street, as the rats didn't like all the flashing lights and noises, and got some kebabs at a fast food joint. I got a "Dantini" and I asked Jake what kind of meat it was.

"That? It's pretty gross. Comes from something called a pig. I hear they're as smart as humans, and eating them is just wrong… Iguana is where it's at." he said, chomping on his iguana kebab.

We sat on a bench in the "park," the bland patch of dirt, and I looked up at the black clouds in the sky. I missed the starlight.

I looked at Jake, and he was staring at me with my chainsaw on my back. "You're the Chainsaw Chick." he said.

"Well, duh. The chainsaw didn't tip you off?" I said.

"Those are common. Every scrapyard in the country has standard issues of those. I thought you just worked there or somethin'. But it's your eyes. In the picture you can hardly see them... but I recognize your red eyes."

"So? Didn't you already kill the 'Chainsaw Chick' when you executed those people?"

"I knew that was just something the politicians cooked up... They hate anything that shows people rebelling. They just want people to eat their iguanas and forget they live in a rat infested Hell on Earth. It's a ruse... but you're not. You're really a serial killer."

"I've killed five demons. Hardly serial killer level."

"All it takes is one killing for you to be a killer."

"...I try to justify it... I try to reason it out in my mind... But it nags at me. When I used to kill in my old, old life, when I was fighting in the arena of the Romans'... I fought just to survive. I was a pit fighter before, like a pitbull dogfighting, fighting other people for other people's sick pleasure. When even I used to fight demons... I gave them mercy, perhaps violent mercy, but mercy nonetheless. Now though... I'm just so angry at the world."

"It's alright to be angry. Fuck, it's *natural* to be angry. The world will kill you. The world will hate you. And demons are just the start. There's nothing to love in the world..."

"There's lots of things to love... Like the ravens."

"The ravens?"

"Yeah... They're carrion birds, but they're so smart and sweet. They make me feel alive."

"Tha'... That's beautiful. That's like the most beautiful, unexpected thing I've ever heard."

I stared into his three eyes, as he stared into my two, and we started kissing each other.

I was kissing this executioner... this carrion bird... and I thought of all the people that die all the time. I wished I could avenge them, as he wished he could feel their pain. I thought of my own death when I-When I died in that car crash.

I stopped kissing and coughed. I realized I was married... married to a man I loved... But the time had passed too long for him to be alive, passed into a futuristic, rat filled dystopia, and I was snagged out of the eternal abyss, while my husband was-

"C'mon babe... we can go home." Jake said, and grinned.

I hit him.

He rubbed his eyes again, as I gave him another black eye, and he said, "Fuck... I was only offering..."

I sighed, and said I'd like to go home.

"Ok. I can walk you there-" he said.

"Not there. To your home." I said.

"Oh! Er. Ok. L-Let's go." he said, and we walked to his home.

He was taking off his shirt in his home, and... every piece of skin was a scar. The only part of him that wasn't his face.

We kissed on the bed. I ran my fingers over every scar... every life that held value...

We laid on the bed, kissing, in each other's embrace...

Then I started strangling him.

He was completely aroused.

I yelled at him, "You *fucker!* You killed thousands of people!! I'm going to let you gasp to death!!"

He couldn't make any sound as I strangled him with my strong hands, but he was fucking smiling.

Smiling.

I angrily looked at him, then released my stranglehold.

He coughed a bit as I sat up, and he said, *"Damn!* That was awesome. Can you just kill me next time?"

"What the fuck is wrong with you?" I asked.

"I don't know. Probably killing people messes me up. But seriously. Do that again." he said.

I put back on my bra, and said, "Next time you won't be alive. I don't want you to die… at least not first feeling your mistakes." I said.

"Don't I show enough penance?" he said.

"No. How could you? A life taken… is a terrible thing." I said.

He sighed, sitting up beside me. He said, "Maybe. Does it matter? They're gone now. How about we take it slow?"

"Fuck off." I said, and walked out the door.

He called out to me, saying, "Just kill me next time."

I slammed the door in anger, and walked down the hall.

I was furiously stalking the streets, chainsaw on my back. That encounter didn't do me any good… I thought it would, I thought it would make me feel like I was really alive, or something… but it just… didn't work.

I found a homeless man begging for change on the side of the street.

The suicidal man from the strip club.

I said to him, "What happened to you, Lucius?? Your *clothes…* They're shredded!!"

He grimaced, and said, "Oh, it's you… It was the rats. They caught me when I didn't expect it. I thought I was safe… but those fuckers can sneak through any barrier. What do *you* want? Can't you see I'm suffering enough?"

"P-Please. Let me help you." I said.

He looked at me warily, and said, "Give me a smile."

"Ok." I said. I smiled nicely, and he took a picture of me.

Then he ran off down the alley, as I called out to him.

I sighed angrily…

And went back to Dina's.

14

The next day, I saw my picture on a billboard, flying my way to work.

Lucius's picture was a nice one, but I guess I was a spokeswoman for some new brand of chips… "Makes you as happy as her!" the slogan said.

Hmph. Maybe at least he won't be doing so badly off for himself, if they at least paid him for the photo…

The strip club was as busy as usual, at all hours strangely enough, but I heard yelling in the back. I looked at Tom the bouncer by the door, and he was staring stonily into the distance… but he did look a little nervous.

Curious, I walked into the back office, and when I opened the door, someone threw a teacup to the floor, and said, "No, Grandma! I'm breaking through the fifth wall with my knowledge!"

"I told you *never* to call me that." Missus M said, "You're poisoning yourself with voodoo and superstition. I'm putting you on leave until you sort yourself out."

"Fuck you, then!! I won't be around to come back! I'm breaking through to the ecological specters! I *quit!*" Dina said.

"*What??* You can't quit! I own you! Ever since you were little you had no one but me!" Missus M said.

Dina stormed out the door, pushing past me.

Missus M sighed, and said, "Good riddance."

"Something wrong?" I said.

"You should be working. But sit, you and Dina are close... Tell me where she got this insane nonsense like 'ecological specters.'" Missus M said.

I sat on the chair in the office, and said, "Um... She does do a lot of drugs..."

"I know that. I've been trying to wean her off of them ever since she went on that crazy psychedelic binge when she was a teen. God... Those were hard days... She'd write crazy shit all over her room, and really liked nonsense books like Lovecraft..." Missus M said, sipping at her tea.

"So you're really Dina's grandma?" I asked.

"No. If anything, I'm her great aunt. We have no blood relation. I absolutely despise that matriarchal name and tone she uses when she calls me 'Grandma...' Her real mother sold her to the milk factories when Dina first started growing breasts, and I gave her a place under my roof instead. She now works for me, as I gave her a place as an employee under me as well." Missus M said.

"Do you want me to talk to her? I don't want her going off the deep end either." I said.

"Yes. I don't need another worker losing themselves to their goddamn selves... Please do, no matter what her choice is for her employment." Missus M said.

I nodded, and charged after Dina who put on her coat over her stripper clothes, and charged out the door.

I found her walking through the alley on her way home, but suddenly, she burst out crying and slumped against the wall.

I went up to her, crouching beside her as she was shaking in tears, and asked her, "What's up? Are you ok?"

She said, "I-I can see past the veil. I can see through the barrier... I can see..."

"It's ok. I think you just need a little rest, just like Missus M said." I said.

"No, Yule. I can see through the veil. You were an angel of Heaven. You fell to Earth for a very selfish reason, to live life again, but instead of being damned as soon as you hit the ground… You caused more good with your life. You had a great life, one I could never have. You had a husband. You had a family. And you were blessed.

"Now you're alone. You're stuck in this Hell on Earth with people like me. You're trapped forever in a limbo life.

"And I love you, but you don't love me. As soon as I saw you I was in love. But you only love the dead as you were.

"I can see all this. I can see past the veil. I can show you…" she said.

She looked into my eyes.

And her eyes turned black, as black as her hair, as black as the clouds.

She kissed me as she stared into my eyes with those black ones.

I felt like I was looking past the grave, past death and life and Heaven and Hell… through the veil of existence, as she kissed me with her eyes open.

I did not want to see this everything underneath the skin of life.

I broke lips with her. She blinked. Her eyes turned their normal color.

And she shut her eyes and cried.

We went back to Dina's home, and I called Missus M, telling her I was taking care of Dina. I said she was a little sick. Missus M told me I better take care of her until Dina is better, or she'll make me wear even less next time I come in.

I just fed Dina lizard noodle soup, while Cass hugged her on the couch. Dina was just staring at the TV… but the TV wasn't on.

Doug barked at Dina once, and Dina looked at him, and said, "I'm sorry that they cut off your balls."

Doug whined.

"It'll be alright, sweetheart…" Cass said to Dina as she was hugging her.

"Nothing matters anymore. I've broken through every barrier- seen through every veil-" Dina said.

"Wanna listen to some music?" I said.

Dina shrugged.

I turned on the radio, with some sort of pop rock playing. "This'll make you feel better!" I said, as I turned it up.

Dina put her face in her hands, and groaned. She removed her hands and said to me, "It must've been so nice in Heaven as an angel like you..." but you're just a ghost now. Just another lost piece of trash like us."

Cass said, "Listen here! We are valuable because Jesus loves us! She sure doesn't look like a ghost, either! C'mon... Just settle down and relax. Want a massage?"

Dina said, "I just want- I don't want- Nothing matters..."

Seeing whatever she showed me, *all the time* I would feel like I was losing it too. But Dina could still be saved.

I decided I'd help talk her out of that strange, crazy feeling. So I talked with her. I started with something good for the mind, something even nostalgic.

I said, "Where did you first hear Spawn of Sax?"

"Huh? I heard him when I was a teen. Grandma got me a radio... and I just listened to the thing constantly. I knew all his songs by heart... He had nothing new for me, but when I started using drugs... It was like I heard everything new again." Dina said.

"Missus M took care of you then, didn't she? Is she a good grandma?" I said.

"She's a bitch. But she does... care, I think. I know what you're think- ing, that she probably forced me into my life... but... I was always a... slut... And being a stripper, it just... came too easy." Dina said.

"Don't say that." I said, "It's just another form of work."

"All those people I've fucked… All those idiots… I feel like I wasted my entire life…" Dina said.

"Hm. Sometimes it's best not to dwell on the past. What do you want to do for the future? Keep your hopes up!" I said.

"I want to die." Dina said.

"Oh… I don't want you to." I said.

Cass hugged Dina, and Doug licked Dina's hand.

Cass started kissing Dina, trying to snap her out of it, but Dina didn't seem very into it. She just sat there and let Cass kiss her. Cass stopped after a bit, and just held her hand.

"What's something that makes you happy? Want me to make some tea?" I said.

"Stop it, Yule. You're not going to snap me out of this with one conversation." Dina said.

"Ok… I want some tea, so I'm going to make you some anyway. So there." I said, and made some tea.

I served it to her, and she just sipped at it. At least she was drinking something.

Frustrated that I couldn't get Dina to realize she was valuable and loved, I just got a beer and drank on the couch next to Cass, Dina, and Doug.

I was soon drunk, and Dina was still mopey. I said, "Heeey… I think I was finally able to copy that dance you do, Dina. Wanna see? Maybe you can give me some tips."

I did a dance before Dina, taking off my shirt, twirling it and throwing it to the side, as we listened to the music. I soon was in nothing but my underwear, swinging my hips before Dina's wide eyes. I flapped my wings at certain times to accentuate certain moves, and I think it came out nicely. I smiled to myself, thinking that this was probably some people's dream, to have an angel strip before them.

Dina said, "You gotta twerk it more at that one part. One more time."

So I got dressed, and did my rehearsal again.

"Whooph. Ok. I feel better." Dina said, "Now... Wanna do it?"

I smiled and kissed her on the cheek. I said, "No, but I'm happy you're feeling better."

Dina smiled, and said, "If you ever need help with anything else... let me know. I think... that actually gave me a certain bit of happiness, yeah. People don't understand... What we do... It's *art*."

"I totally agree. I mean, not always, sometimes I feel like a slut turning a trick, but hey, it can be artful." I said, "That's why I prefer to draw on people's happiness in other ways, but if you really enjoy what you do, then you should keep doing it."

"Yeah... I bet Grandma will be sore as hell when I come back... But I think I could manage it, if I saw you there." Dina said.

Cass said, "Great! Now, you've probably had a long day... Let me massage you *properly* this time. You just need to relax."

"O-Ok. I'll try to relax. I don't feel so fucked up now..." Dina said, as Cass led her to the bedroom.

I watched TV in my underwear with Doug and downed more beers. Just random crap on the TV, ridiculous shows of the time, and I was feeling happy, pretty drunk.

But then there was static on the screen.

It sounded like someone was screaming from the static, in horrible, angry agony.

My goosebumps stood up ten times, as the scream just continued.

Then it was the nature documentary again, following the last lion on Earth, which was black.

The poor lion... it was starved, malnourished, but the people spoke of it like it was something beautiful, like they were treating it the best in the world. It was in a cage, with no plant life at all.

Then the "tamer" came in. She was a demon, and she commanded the lion to do tricks for the viewers. The stupid humans just laughed and applauded as the last lion rolled over for them.

Fuck them all. Fuck them all to Hell.

15

Dina just worked the bar at the strip club now, but she enjoyed watching me take up her position on the pole. I always did her routine, with my own happy twists, and people really enjoyed my show. It was just entertainment, even though some may think it's raunchy.

I never thought I would have such an idea of strip clubs before… I never went to one in my past life, in truth. Sure, my husband had once, but only when he had just turned 21. He told me he really wasn't into the whole thing, as he preferred when women took his money with a drink and at least had a decent conversation with him first, instead of dancing like bimbos. I tried to continue what he would've liked with other people here, drinks and conversation.

And I took off my sexy stripper top too, as the people cheered.

I was having my lunch in the break room, and Dina said from across from me, "You're killing it out there! We're going to have to reserve you for special occasions or some shit! Keep it up." I smiled.

I was walking home, just to enjoy a different horizon than from the air, and a man with no ears was waiting for me in an alley.

He clicked a button, and sound came from a speaker he was holding.

"Is it on? Oh. Hello, my little rascal. I wanted to talk to you." the woman in the speaker, Daemonia, the cartel ringleader from before, said.

I said, "Stay the fuck away from me, from Lux, and everyone."

"Oh, don't worry, I don't hold a grudge with you for beating the shit out of some of my men... In fact, they've all been disposed of properly now. No. I want to make a deal."

"...What do you want?"

"I've noticed you've been making rises in the news... Chainsaw Chick. Ever since you resurfaced at that prison and escaped, you've chalked up nearly one hundred murders. Someone like you could come in handy."

"I don't know what you're talking about." I said, crossing my arms.

"Come, let's take a walk. Surely we can help each other out..." she said. The earless man waved to me to follow him.

We walked down the street, as the woman gabbed on about a new suit she ordered, made from the last lion that was alive.

I said, "I thought you were a computer."

"I am! That's what makes buying a suit so fantastically rich. I don't even need it! Hahaha!" she said.

"...Um. Can we cut to the chase?"

"Sure. There is someone important I want you to assassinate. Some-one special... That I know only you will be able to get to. He's up high, in that huge, black tower. Made. Just. For. Him. I need you to get rid of him... permanently. When you do, my rival in the electric market will plummet back down to Hell, where he belongs, and I can finally break into power with my new brand of baby human electricity." she said.

"Baby human electricity?"

"Something about babies... I haven't worked out the details yet. But my scientists guarantee we should be able to harvest them for power."

"...You make me sick."

"Oh, come now. Babies didn't even get a life yet, and they won't grow up... very long. It is nothing different than abortion. Cut the life short, before they have any sort of life at all. And there is just an appalling amount of overpopulation today."

"Why? Why would I ever help you?"

"Glory. Riches. Everything you could desire. I could make you a queen. You look like an angel, and I will take you to Heaven, if you only kill one... *thing...*"

"No. I don't want your wealth. I don't need it, don't want it, won't have it."

"Hmmm. Then perhaps... You need to understand the full scope. It was worth a shot trying to tempt you. I believe you need to talk to my rival... and understand what he is harvesting."

"And then kill your rival?"

She laughed, and said, "No, dear. Just talk. He is the human scientist/ entrepreneur who is technically keeping this entire city running. Keeping the entire country running. Selling off unlimited electricity for the entire world. He improved harvesting demons *so* much... that only one of them needs to be harvested now. Talk to him. Learn what you need to know... and then do what I ask."

The earless man shut off the speaker, and walked away, as I asked her what she meant.

16

I smoked a cigarette outside of Lux's home, looking at the streetlight flickering.

I thought I heard that scream again, but I think it was just the insects buzzing around.

I flicked my cigarette butt, and went inside to Lux.

"I'm still pissed at you, you know." I said.

He poured a vial of something into a mixture, and said, "I know… but I suppose this whole experiment is a whole mess of a project, anyway. I suppose having an angel that's a ghost was a foolish project to even begin with…"

"Would you mind calling me by my name and not 'angel,' 'ghost,' or 'experiment? Do you even know what my full name is?"

"Not really. Does it matter? If you want to introduce yourself, then that's fine by me." he said, and swirled the mixture around.

"My name is Yule Tidings."

"Like some sort of Christmas carol? You could be more creative than *that*…"

"You don't like Christmas? You some sort of Grinch?"

"What's a Grinch?"

"A nasty creature who doesn't like happiness and joy… Looks kinda like you, actually, if he was metal and not fuzzy."

"...And you look like a snarky angel to me. Alright, Yule, I suppose that works."

"Thanks. What do you know about that scientist/entrepreneur who makes this city's power?"

Lux accidentally crushed a vial in his hand he was picking up, and corrosive acid spilled everywhere, all down his arm.

He wiped the acid off, and said, "He is nothing but another thief, taking SSS's work and using it for himself. He makes me ashamed to even try and improve on her theories... but I needed to try and give her a good name."

"Why? I thought you hated her or something for making you a sex robot."

"I... I didn't, at the start... It was a very intimate relationship. But in the end, I was just another toy."

"Ooooh. I get it. You were jealous of her lover or something!"

"Er... Not all of them... None of them could remotely come up to my strength! Or my intellect! Or my parts! They had teeny tiny little things, and I was as huge as-" he started.

"It's alright. I was only kidding. I never expected a robot to be jealous before."

Lux sighed, and said, "I really did try to make her happy, Yule. But I was just a toy."

I shrugged, and said, "At least it wasn't totally a one sided love."

"I suppose. Anyway, I hope you don't die anytime soon, because... I'm really interested to see how far you take the Chainsaw Chick."

"I... I, uh, never killed hundreds of people and only-"

"I don't care if you kill millions, Yule. But it seems to give you purpose."

"...Thanks, I think. Well, I'm off to the pub. See ya, Lux."

I drank wine with Jake, and asked him also what he knew about that scientist/entrepreneur.

We just got drinks every now and then. I suppose I could've picked a worse drinking buddy.

Jake put a drop of cyanide in his drink, and drank it down. He was working on his tolerance towards cyanide.

"That dude? Some rich bitch. I don't know how he managed to pull off such a heist on the market... He was no one, with even a criminal record I think, but now everyone knows his name." Jake said, as he sipped at his cyanide concoction.

"Er... What's his name?" I asked.

"You know! The one with all the Xs and Zs. I can't really pronounce it, but y'know!" he said.

"Alright." I said, sipping at my wine, "How's work?"

"...Fine. Juuuust fine... Stupid demons are warping my execution poison... They're trading it in the prison black market, instead of letting everyone use it... Fuckers could make executions a sweet thing, but noooo... They tempt prisoners with it, because they want executions to be feared. They don't want to end their miserable lives with a smile... they've gotta draw it out. So it's a special reward if you do everything the demons tell you, suck their cock like they own you... and then they kill you with my poison..." Jake said, grumbling and drinking his cyanide.

"I'm sure you can find a better outlet for peace."

"All I do is keep swinging the axe, all bloody day... with the fucking cheering demons... Sometimes I wish I could move back to the country, and work the scythe again."

"You were a farmer?"

"Yep. It's where I got such a firm swing. Reaping the wheat, chopping wood... Wha'? You didn't notice my badass muscles from the start?" he said, and flexed for me.

"I did. But I know muscles don't make everything about a man. I mean, they're not even that big, really. In comparison to *mine...*" I said, and flexed back at him.

He grinned, and challenged me to a game of arm wrestling, whoever lost had to buy whatever the winner wanted.

I smiled later, as I made him buy Dantini's and eat the pork with me. He stuck his tongue out when he smelled the delicious pig, and slowly took a bite. He chewed on it slowly, swallowed, and said, "You must be sick or somethin', eatin' them poor pigs..."

I just chewed on my pork, and shrugged.

17

Cass and I were taking Doug for a walk, and while we were walking, a demon kicked Doug.

Doug snarled at the demon, jumping and barking at the creature from Hell. Cass tried to hold him back, as the demon laughed.

"Heya, baby. Your mutt probably is sick. Want me to put him down?" the demon said, and wielded a long, cruel looking knife, approaching Doug.

"You stay away from him, if you know what's good for you." Cass said.

"I'm gonna kill your little puppy, robo bitch..." the demon said.

"Doug! Stay." Cass said, and Doug sat down beside Cass, and Cass let go of the leash.

Then Cass relentlessly started beating the shit out of the demon. The demon was shocked, as he dropped his knife, and Cass just mercilessly beat him within an inch of his life.

The demon had broken arms and was laying on his side in a gutter soon, and Cass said, "Learn not to mess with people's pets, demon." She grabbed up Doug's leash and we continued our walk.

"I thought you didn't want to avenge yourself?" I said.

"Oh, I was just showing the proper manners. When someone messes with someone you care for, you mess with them... It's the polite thing to do." Cass said.

"I don't know how you're not doing that to every demon you see, with what they did to you. I'd be so mad if someone took my arms and legs…"

"I'm working on forgiveness and good habits. It's not good for your mind to dwell on pain of the past. Even Doug listens when I tell him something, and won't jump off the leash if commanded. He knows some habits are worth breaking."

"But… it's not like demons belong here or anything. They should all be in Hell…"

"You could learn something from Doug, Yule. He could hold a grudge against all humans, for what they did to him, but then he would simply be a wild animal, ripping people apart for merciless vengeance. And what kind of life to live is that? No, it is better to be at peace with the world and yourself." Cass said.

"I suppose…" I said. We passed by a gang of men who hooted and whooped at us, and we tried to ignore them. But then one stepped in front of us, smoking a cigarette. He had a long goatee and seven fingers on each hand. Doug was growling at him.

He said, "Hey… It's the chick who took Amare's arm. Pleased to meet you, ladies. I'm Vindicta. You probably saw me on the news, once, twice, or all the time. I'm their main star! I've got bounties on my head from here to Europe, and everyone knows me…"

"I've never heard of you, Vindicta." I said.

His grin left him, and he said, "You obviously are some sort of shut in then. Anyway… I noticed you walking my dog. How's Dina doing?"

"You know Dina?" Cass said.

"We dated for a year. And then the bitch stole my dog… All I wanted was her to show off her bod for the guys and give them a good fuck… But no… Fuckin' slut prefers dogs, I guess." Vindicta said.

"So you're her asshole ex. She told me about you, and just so you know, she *prefers* people who don't strangle her with their stupid seven fingered hands. People like me." Cass said, frowning at the man.

Vindicta said, "What?? She's had so much dick she doesn't even want it anymore?? Guys! Listen to this bitch! She's fucking my old lady scissor style! Man... I wish I could see that!" and they all laughed.

They then all hooted at us, and called us butches and dikes, and I grabbed Cass by the arm as we tried to continue walking.

But Cass stopped, with an angry expression on her face.

She told Doug to stay, and dropped the leash.

Then she walked over to Vindicta.

Vindicta said, "You had enough pussy and need some cock, sweetie?"

Cass smashed Vindicta on the face with her robotic fist.

Vindicta's gang pulled their guns at Cass, but Vindicta rubbed his bleeding nose, and said, "No, guys. Let me take on this little chickie. She's never fucked with *Vindicta* before..."

The two circled each other with their fists raised, ready to throw the second punch.

Vindicta feinted with a swing, which Cass was going to block, and then he whacked Cass in the kidney with a seven knuckled punch.

Cass grunted in pain, and Vindicta whacked her again and again in the face, left, right, left.

Then Vindicta started strangling Cass with fourteen fingers.

But Cass jammed her robotic hands on his arm joints, breaking the stranglehold, and screamed out, "Our Father who art in Heaven!!"

Then she whammed Vindicta over and over, never letting him have a chance to block, too furiously fast for anyone to defend against.

The blunted sound of Cass's metallic fists whumping on flesh sounded through the street.

And with one more uppercut, Vindicta was left lying on the street.

His gang all looked at Vindicta, and one of them said, "Knew his winning streak wouldn't last forever. Let's go, guys."

The gang walked down the street, leaving Vindicta unconscious, barely alive.

Cass picked up Doug's leash, and we continued our walk, her happily smiling and whistling, after mercilessly getting vengeance on Vindicta.

18

I was walking home again, and I heard a strange noise coming from an alley. It sounded like flute music. I walked down the alley, and saw someone playing for a crowd... a crowd of rats.

Lucius played a soothing sound to the rodents, and when he was done, the rats scampered away down the gutters again. He turned to me, and said, "Hello."

"You're alive!! Thank God. So... You've picked up some musical talents?" I said.

"Thank you for that photo. I was able to trade it along with my phone for this pipe from a pawnshop. I really only wanted something to enjoy, like music, but it seems the rats enjoy it too."

"That's... interesting! Good for you. Do you need any more help with anything?" I asked.

He shook his head, and said, "I've been thinking about your words, and all I really want... is a colorful flower. I think if I keep living I'll be able to see one, a real one, someday."

"Great. Maybe I can just give you some cash? So you can buy dinner or something?" I said.

"Hmm... I would like something the rats haven't scavenged for me... They give me gifts sometimes. What about- a- cheeseburger??" he said.

"Sure, c'mon." I said, and we went to a local fast food joint.

Lucius didn't know what to order, picking number six, then number one, then number three, and so on. So I said we'll take every number he wanted.

He devoured the six cheeseburgers in no time, as I ate one across from him. I never knew they could make lizard burgers taste so *almost* like the real thing.

He was crying tears of delight, eating the burgers, and said with a stuffed mouth, "They don't make better food than a normal cheeseburger. Those rich snobs... all they eat are caviar and beef. Pathetic. They'll never be down to earth like us, with tasty monitor burgers with some good ol' gecko nuggets. They don't know what they're missing. Like that one guy, with that crazy X's and Z's name. No one so removed from society than him. I hear all he does is sit in that giant tower of his and do who knows what."

"Hm? What do you think he does?" I asked, chomping on my burger.

"Probably forbidden experiments. Or maybe he just sits alone and masturbates. I don't know. Strange, that he would have such a hidden passage so out in the open... Y'know? I thought secrets were supposed to be secret, but I see him sometimes, just hopping into that manhole like nothing. I would never do something so stupid as that... Even though I've got an understanding with the rats, I'd never encroach on their turf." he said.

"What? Where's this secret manhole?" I asked.

"Down on 11th avenue. The first one by the intersection." he said, "Well, thanks for the burgers. I think I'll be able to sleep like nothing else tonight. Goodnight."

"Goodnight. Stay safe, Lucius!" I said, as he wandered out the door, a homeless pied piper.

I checked out this manhole Lucius told me about. It looked like a normal manhole. I raised the lid, and descended into the darkness with my chainsaw.

I heard the rats snickering at me, laughing in their diabolical way, for I was in their world now.

I saw thousands of eyes watching me, everywhere. I jumped when one ran past me, bumping into my boot, and I continued on into the darkness, with nothing but my phone light lighting the way.

It looked like a normal sewer... but there was a door on the wall. I checked it out, and it was locked.

I started up my chainsaw, and worked on destroying the lock.

The rats were immediately all drawn to the sound of my chainsaw, they were everywhere, waiting, watching, and I was sweating nervously as they circled me.

The lock was soon broken, and I quickly opened the door and got inside, then shut the door before the rats could attack.

I heard them squeaking and scratching at the door, trying to force it open, but I held it closed fast.

I saw a metal chair, and I propped it against the door, keeping it shut. I sighed in relief as I soon heard the rats lose interest and wander away, even though I knew they'd be waiting.

I looked around this room, and saw a shrine.

I approached it... and it was a shrine to Jesus Christ, with family photos of a man littering the scene.

Paul. The singer of Spawn of Sax... my friend, whom I sometimes thought of as a nephew.

Wait... this wasn't Paul. The man looked almost exactly like him, but he had no scar on his face like Paul had... and had a different sort of smile. Plus he had an extra incisor in all his photos of him smiling.

Someone lit a cigarette, and Paul walked out of the shadows.

"Heya, Yule. How are you these days?" he said, walking in front of the shrine, in front of me.

"Are you really Paul??" I said.

"My name is Zaxazaxar. And I don't like you defiling my sanctuary." he said.

"How do you know my name?" I asked.

He shrugged, and said, "Your story is told countlessly by my family. Yours, Paul's, everyone you knew. My ancestor is quite a legend, and the angel that gave my family a second chance is quite renowned. But... I didn't believe a word of it, until you just admitted who you are."

"I see you follow Jesus." I said.

"I am probably the most devout man in the world. Only *I...* could've defeated God's immortal enemy. Only *I...* knew what to do." he said.

"What do you mean?" I asked.

He turned to the shrine of Jesus, and said with his back to me, "This man... He sacrificed himself for the world. As Paul did. But not you. You let Paul die, you let the world suffer. I believe in Jesus almost to a fault... but I do not believe in the rest of his followers." He clenched his fists angrily, and said, "All the angels... they are nothing but a disgrace. Even God's first betrayed him... Even you betrayed Paul. Even God let Jesus die. The world today is not ruled by God... it is ruled by men, like Jesus Christ."

"But... Jesus is God..." I said.

He turned back, and said, "No. Jesus was just a man, raised to some hogwash prophecy. Raised to legends. Just like Paul. My family has kept him alive through ages... a dead man, a damned man... but he lives on through us. And our enemies are kept close to our hearts as well. You, Yule, are Judas Iscariot to my family."

"No! I truly did try to save Paul! I couldn't even approach the church he died in because the flames were too-" I started.

"Enough. I wish for you to suffer as he did… In flames. Now die, Yule. Die in fire." he said.

He threw the cigarette at me, and threw a fireball from his hand. A large fireball from some sort of device attached to his wrist, and it hit me in the face. Lightning crackled from the blast, and it shocked and burned me. I could not move, I felt my eyesight flicker and fade, and I collapsed on the ground.

I was unconscious and screaming in agony in this dream. I felt like I was in Hell… I felt like I was in Heaven… but torn to pieces, in both worlds, just endlessly shifting realms, unable to see the light… unable to live in the darkness… and so alone.

I woke up, and opened my eyes.

But I couldn't see the world around me. All I could see was fire.

I screamed as my eyes burned, I tried to rub off the flames, but my hands were engulfed in fire too.

I was ablaze, my clothes burned to nothing, my wings were scorched, gone, and I was burning to ash, like a demon of Hell.

Even *I* did not belong here.

I looked at the shrine to Jesus, my friend, and I prayed… for a quick end to this suffering.

I felt a feeling of peace, as I was in so much pain.

I saw Max, about to welcome me into death.

But Max said, as he held my burning hand, "I want you to continue your life."

The pain stopped.

I looked down at my hands, burning, the flesh was singed and seared… but the flames did not consume me fully.

I raised myself up from the ground, and stumbled out the opened door of this sanctuary.

I dropped into the sewer water, rolling in the muck, drenching the flames in filth, and passed out.

The rats were gnawing on me when I awoke again, chewing at my flesh.

I screamed out, and the rats scampered away for a second, before attacking my body again.

I tried to rip them off of me, tearing at them attached to me with fangs.

I ran down the sewers, my burnt flesh hurting, bleeding from the claw and teeth marks, the rats chasing me.

I saw the manhole tunnel entrance blocked by a wall of rodents, so I continued on down another path, into the darkness.

I just ran and ran, crying and hurting.

I prayed for light.

My hand started sparking, and sparking, and lit into flame again.

I screamed again, looking at my burning hand, but the rodents stayed away from the flame.

I raised my burning hand at the enemy, at the rats, as they circled me everywhere.

"Enough!! Leave me alone!!" I screamed out.

The rats snickered.

But I heard a sound of something peaceful up above. The sound of a flute. I ran to that sound, keeping the rats back with my burning hand.

I quickly climbed a ladder up a manhole, as the rats attacked my naked feet, shoes and clothes gone.

I sobbed, as I pushed open the lid, and rolled over to the side of the manhole.

The rats were trying to drag me back into the sewer by my feet, but someone held my hand and dragged me away.

Lucius looked down at me, shocked, and said, "Holy shit!! Are you alive??"

"Th-Thank you. Thank you so much... Thank you." I said.

He carried me away, as it started raining, the water dousing my burns and flaming hand, and I looked up at his worried face one last time... and then I passed out again.

Lucius carried me to the strip club, and Missus M immediately shut down the place and got me attended to in a bed in the back.

Tom checked my wounds and bandaged me up. I thanked him, and I asked him if he knew what he was doing. Tom said, "I used to be in the army. I know how it feels to hurt, and I know how to fix it."

Tom was very professional to my naked body, as professional as he always was, and he applied burn cream everywhere and bandaged up the bite marks.

The other girls all kept me company, watching me and talking with me. They tried to cheer me up as best they could. Suzy, the woman with four breasts, kept telling me these silly jokes, and I kept laughing at her silliness, even though it hurt to laugh. She was trying to break through as a comedian. Dina just watched me sadly at my bedside.

Lucius watched me from afar, but I beckoned him closer and told him I wanted to say something to him.

He knelt before me, and put his ear to my lips.

I kissed his cheek softly.

He looked back at me and smiled.

"I guess we're even now. You saved my life... I saved yours." he said.

"Yeah. If you ever need... *anything...* I am yours." I said.

"I want you to keep living, just so you can see those flowers with me." he said.

I smiled.

I spent a long time in that bed. Lux soon came by and worked on me, doing all sorts of advanced medical procedures on me. Tom wouldn't let him take me away though, because I was his patient, so the two worked on me together. Cass tried to hug me, but Tom wouldn't let her touch me as I was so burned, so she just sat with me most of the time and fed me some of her cooking. Doug sat by my side night and day, and watched the TV Missus M brought in for me.

It was a little odd being there all burned up during the strip club's working hours. I'd hear the sound of dancing and the other girls using the other beds with their clientele on and off, but I didn't mind it too much. The moans from the other rooms were kind of comforting, anyway, as it sounded like the people were enjoying themselves.

Jake came by to visit, and got me a big bottle of scotch to drink together.

"Toldja the rats are king." Jake said.

"You didn't say that! I said that." I said.

He shrugged, slurping down almost all of my scotch, and said, "Fuck it. Are you fuckin' tryin' to kill yourself or somethin'?? No one goes down to the rats. It's like… survival instincts."

"I needed to know. I needed to understand… but I'm only left with more questions…" I said.

Jake said, "Fuckin' idiot. Just go kill demons from now on, not rats…"

"I think I want to kill Zaxazaxar… but… I don't know why he hates me so much…" I said.

"Hm? That guy did this to you?? Fuckin' hell… I'll kill him myself…" Jake said.

"Don't worry about it. I think I know what I want to do when I get better, though." I said.

"What's that?" Jake said.

"Accept a job." I said.

19

I had no wings. My wings were burned off of me... and my skin itched...

But I was better, mostly. I walked with Lux back to his home, as he said he wanted to show me something.

We got inside, as I limped in after him, and he showed me my chainsaw I had left in the sewers, cleaned off and as powerful as it always was.

I ran a hand down the saw blade. Some things will never leave us, constant companions. A hat, a cat, or a chainsaw.

I thanked Lux, and picked up the saw.

It felt perfectly proportioned to me, the right amount of length, the right weight, and even had a handy strap when I wasn't using it for its true purpose. It felt like a part of me, in a way.

"So. All the great warriors name their weapons. It took forever finding it again down in those sewers... but I think you should name your chainsaw. What do you want to call it, Yule?" Lux asked.

"I want to call it-" I started.

"Dismemberer? Rat Bane? Exorcist? The Apocalypse?" Lux suggested.

"I think I'll just call it a chainsaw. If that's ok! I really don't know what I would call it." I said.

"Oh. Ok, I guess... Well, you mentioned you wanted to find my old business associate... Daemonia is quite a manipulative entity, I do not believe you will be able to trust her." Lux said.

"I need her aid if I am to get into that tower and find out whatever Zaxazaxar is doing. As you can see... I have no wings." I said.

"The nerves aren't hurting you from where they were, are they?" Lux asked.

"I do feel like flapping them sometimes, or like they're still attached. But the wounds have healed well..." I said.

"Well... Me and her... used to talk in a chatroom before. You may be able to meet her on the internet." Lux said.

"Alright. Maybe that's safer, as I won't be in her clutches then."

"Hardly. You need to enter the room mentally. You will be more vulnerable than anything there."

"Oh. Ok... How do I do that?" I asked.

Lux patted the table, and I sat down on it. He said, "For me it is nothing but flipping a switch. For you... We'll need you to eat this nanobot. Don't worry, it passes out of your body like any other food, but while it lasts... you will be able to transcend time and space in the eternal web."

Lux went to his fridge, and got me a chocolate cake.

"Just eat this, lay down, and try to remain calm." Lux said.

I ate the cake, laid down on the table, and Lux tucked me in with the blanket.

I soon felt like I was getting sleepy... and sleepy...

When I woke up- no wait, I think I was asleep.

But things were floating around me, little bugs of all colors, and I wasn't in Lux's home anymore.

I was in a graveyard.

I got up from the coffin, and walked through the tombstones. The tombstones were all blank.

Something slithered behind me, and I turned quickly, but it was gone.

My goosebumps stood up, and I looked up at the sky, which was dark, no it was light, no it was dark, no it was light… something in between.

I walked through the graveyard, hearing the footsteps crunch after me.

I started running, as the thing behind me chased me, through this graveyard which never seemed to end.

I started panicking, scared, afraid of this new setting, no one around me but that thing following me, whatever it was.

The thing cornered me at a dead end in the graveyard, a large fence blocking any escape route.

I turned back to look at the thing, and I was-

Confused?

It was a tiny white rabbit.

"Hello. Welcome to the internet." he said, in a cute tiny voice.

"Huh? Who are you?" I asked.

"I'm Clippers. Your guide. Just pet me if you need help with any-thing!" he said.

"Ok… I need to find Daemonia." I said.

He was silent, so I carefully walked over to him and pet him.

He started buzzing, and said, "There are nearly 400 billion chat rooms with people with demon related usernames frequenting it. Would you like me to take you to all of them?"

"No… Um, she said something about buying a suit made from the last lion." I said.

"There is one virus with that suit. Would you like me to take you to it?" he said.

"Er… Yes." I said.

Clippers hopped at me, and when he hit me, we were somewhere else.

We were in front of a beautiful palace, and a maid came to me quickly and bowed, as I held Clippers.

"We've been expecting you, Miss Chainsaw Chick." the maid said.

"You have?" I said, as she led me through the palace doors.

She was silent, but brought me inside, which looked even bigger than the outside. When we walked into the palace, we were now outside the palace, with a bigger palace in front of us. The maid just kept leading us through palaces, which got more and more opulent and bigger every time. I asked, "How long is this going to go on?"

"Just until you fully appreciate the majesty of my master." the maid said.

"I get it. She's very rich." I said.

"Good. It would behoove you to know who your betters are." the maid said.

Then the maid snapped her fingers, and we were in a lounge. She offered me a drink, and said, "The best, most inebriating data of the net. Have a drink."

"No thanks. I think I'd just like to get down to business. How long do I have to wait?" I asked.

"Just until you fully understand the generosity of your master." she said.

"My master?" I asked.

"Why, *me* of course!" the maid said, and started laughing. She slurped at the drink she was offering me, and lounged on the sofa. "I love this gag. The old servant is the master trick. I serve myself, thus I am master. You will be serving me."

"Oh. Hello, Daemonia." I said.

"Want to watch TV? It's a special program that I'm *dying* to see end." Daemonia said.

She clicked on the huge TV with a wave of her hand, and I saw... a dying demon woman, attached to tubes and wires. She looked utterly lifeless, but her heart rate monitor still beeped out that she was alive.

"My original. She comes back to Earth, again and again, but she never gets what she wants… This time she tried to make a backup of herself, but all she got… was me. I love seeing her suffer in agony! She knows I'm watching her, constantly… and there's nothing she can do about it. Ha!" Daemonia said.

"Um. I've dealt with her before in a past life… and I know she is not to be trifled with. Just as I know not to trifle with you." I said.

"Wise. So what *is* it you want?"

"I want to accept your job, and follow through with it."

"Excellent. And I suppose now you need my aid as well? I noticed you're wingless now."

"Yes. I need to know everything about how to get into that tower."

She said, "The only way in is through a small window on the very, very top. It's why I needed your wings… and only one person with enough skill to pull off this assassination. Too many people will alert every godawful ounce of security in that place… How do you have the qualifications to do this?"

"I could climb?"

"Impossible. You'd take days of climbing, on a sleek surface. Go ahead, if you want. Your life doesn't really mean anything to me."

"You can't help me at all?" I asked.

"I can help myself. You should do the same. If you really need a suggestion… Burn through the clouds." she said, slurped down the rest of the data drink, and continued, "Now I am really curious about whatever else you can give me, so I'm going to probe your mind for a second."

"What? No." I said.

She grinned, and said, "Just relax… That's the most important bit… Welcome to Friendliness, chump…"

She was already in my mind, stealing bits of info of my life.

I started panicking, as she looked at me, probing my life just by looking at me.

I felt her creeping tendrils everywhere in me, all across my body. It felt like she was touching me forcefully with her mind.

She was ripping off my attire, looking at my bare psyche naked.

She looked at the pure essence of my mind, admiring it for a second.

I knew soon I would be Daemonia, if I didn't escape.

I looked back at the TV, and the dying demon woman named Darcy sighed at me.

I pet Clippers, and said, "Take me home."

"To the home page we go." he said.

We poofed back into the graveyard, as I heard the echo of Daemonia laughing at me.

I just kept petting Clippers as I sat by the coffin. I didn't need any more help with anything, but this bunny was rather soothing.

I set Clippers beside the coffin, got in, and went back to sleep, where I would wake up.

20

I woke up on the table with Lux watching me.

But also with Clippers beside me.

"Clippers?" I said.

Lux said, "Huh? You must be hallucinating. It takes a while for the nanobot to wear off. Here, I made you some coffee so you can wake up, and use the bathroom so you can expel the nanobot."

The bunny just hopped around in the air as I stared at it.

I drank coffee and chatted with Lux about Daemonia, the virus, and watched Clippers fly around beside me.

"Burn through the clouds?" Lux said.

"I don't know." I said.

"Hmm... Anyway, just take a rest for a bit. You've been through a lot."

"Thank you, Lux. I think I'm going to hang out with my new best friend, my friend who pulled me away from the rats." I said, and was about to walk out the door, but went to hug Lux, and then picked up the chainsaw, holstering it on my back.

I found Lucius playing for a crowd of people this time, and he was accepting tips for his music. He actually was starting to get rather good at the flute, and had some new clothes that weren't shredded. I sat down before him with the other people, and let him play for us.

I clapped when he was done, and he bowed to us.

I approached him, and I said, "Heya, Lucius! How are you?"

"Just fine, Yule. How are you?" he said.

"I'm just enjoying the music. You've gotten great!"

He smiled, and said, "I never expected my life to take such a turn, after I decided to continue living. It's a nice feeling."

I smiled, and said, "Wanna get some burgers?"

"Sure!" he said and smiled.

We ate the burgers, joking and laughing, and I told him all about different colored flowers.

"You mean… cornflowers aren't black?" Lucius said.

"Nope! They're blue!" I said, and smiled.

"And petunias… Not black?" he said.

"They can be every color of the rainbow, actually." I said.

"Really?? I never knew *any* flower could be more than one color!" he said, and smiled.

I giggled, and said, "It's quite a sight. I can't wait until we find them."

We looked into each other's eyes, smiling.

I thought it was a nice little date, but I didn't tell Lucius that.

Even though Clippers kept flying around beside me. I shrugged the flying digital bunny off and ate gecko nuggets with barbeque sauce.

I kept thinking of Lucius as I walked home. I suppose if you save a gal's life then it is hard for her to stop thinking about you.

I giggled to myself at a bad joke he made earlier, and continued walking, skipping for a ways. Clippers hopped along beside me.

I stopped with Clippers and looked at the huge tower pushing through the clouds. If only I could fly…

I skipped along again for a while, and then I started smelling something odd.

Smoke. I looked down and my clothes were smoldering.

I screamed, and tried dropping and rolling, but my clothes still smoldered. I quickly took off my clothes, my shirt, my pants…

It wasn't my clothes that were smoldering. It was me.

I screamed, and ran down the streets, naked and smoking.

My arms and legs started sparking, and sparking, and ignited into flame.

Why?! Not again, please God, not again!

I got to Lux's door, pounding on the door as my fists burned, screaming for Lux to help me.

He quickly let me in, and wrapped me in a wet blanket.

I shivered at the cold, but at least I didn't feel so hot anymore.

"Are you ok?" Lux said.

"I start smoking, and then I start burning. Please help me." I said.

"Just… Just sit tight." Lux said, and then quickly began rummaging in the fridge.

I shivered from the cold… and I kept on getting warmer and warmer. I dreaded that heat.

Lux soon offered me clothes.

Cold clothes, that were chill to the touch. I quickly put them on, and I didn't feel like I was getting warmer anymore. I was just wrapped in cold, and I sighed in relief.

"Have you been touching demon electricity?" Lux asked.

"What? What's that?" I asked.

"The power of a soul is electrifying… the power of a demon's soul burns. It will keep on burning until it consumes every ounce of fuel you have. It is quite a remarkable power source, but it is extremely dangerous. If humans touch it the flame lingers, until you burn to ash… Some cases have lived *pretty* long, if treated properly, but for most… They do not last the week." Lux said.

"Is that why you gave me these cold clothes?" I said.

"They should keep you cool until I can improve a better design. If you take them off you could combust at any second, so stay clothed."

"Dang… I was really getting good at taking them off, too… Oh well. This is a bit terrifying to me. Is there any way to cure myself?"

"No one has found a way to remove the fire. You could talk with some of the cases that have touched the fire in the hospital, in case you're wondering what awaits you."

"…Alright. I'll do that. Thank you for everything."

"No problem. And Yule…" Lux said, as I was about to walk out the door, "Don't talk to the white rabbit."

I turned back, and saw Clippers sitting on Lux's shoulder.

"Why not?" I said.

"It means the nanobot is still festering in you. I looked up the name 'Clippers,' and apparently that's a very old program that a company made to help people traverse the internet." Lux said.

Clippers hopped into my arms, and I started petting him. I said, "Sounds like a good guy, to me."

"Er… that was its intent, to be a good program… but you see, everyone got so annoyed by it that the company deleted it from all its software and basically buried it in a digital graveyard. You seeing it still isn't a good sign. It could be a virus, or perhaps malware in a recognizable form… I'd try to let it pass if I was you."

I looked down at Clippers, who was wiggling his nose. I placed him on the ground beside me and shrugged.

Still, when I left, closing the door and leaving Clippers and Lux, Clippers was in the alley beside me and hopped next to me on my way to the hospital.

This rabbit didn't look extremely evil in any way. Just looked like a white rabbit.

Clippers started buzzing, and said, "You have two hundred new notifications. Would you like to check them all?"

"Er, no thanks. How do I have notifications? I've only used the internet once." I said.

"Forty new accounts were made for you when you logged on. Would you like to delete them?" Clippers said.

"Sure." I said.

Clippers buzzed, and said, "Sorry, unable to delete. You have 4000 new emails from your cousins, sisters, brothers, mothers, fathers, boyfriends and girlfriends. Would you like to open them all?"

"All my family is dead. And how can I have multiple mothers and fathers?"

Clippers buzzed some more, and said, "Urgent. Your mother wants to know your mother's maiden name. She is in the hospital with a bad case of prostate cancer."

"That doesn't make any sort of sense."

"Would you like to listen to some music?"

"Huh. That sounds fine, Clippers."

A soothing sort of music came on from Clippers, and I smiled and relaxed walking down the street, but the music quickly stopped in the middle of the song and played an ad.

I was frowning as I walked into the hospital. Clippers was annoying the crap out of me. I tried to tell him to be silent, but he just played a song called "Silent" instead.

I told the hospital receptionist I'd like to visit someone who was infected by demon electricity, as I too was infected by it.

She did a double take at me, and said, "What? You need to be treated right away!! How are you still walking around and talking?? Most don't live the week!"

"Er, I am being treated! See, feel my clothes." I said. She nervously put a hand to my clothed arm, expecting me to burst into flame at any second, and felt the cold.

"...I can schedule you to see a real doctor, if you like? I don't know how clothes you put in the fridge can keep you safe..." the receptionist said.

"Oh, no worries. I know someone who can get me all sorted out. I'd really just like to talk to other people who are going through the same thing." I said.

"...Go to the burning ward. I warn you... it's cold." she said. She gave me directions, and I thanked her.

I walked into the "burning ward," and it was like I walked into a freezer. I looked through windows at patients, and they were all wrapped in cold, wet blankets, keeping them freezing. Most had no patch of skin exposed.

But I saw one girl writing on a whiteboard with a marker, peacefully in her room. She looked at me and smiled. I smiled and waved to her. She put the whiteboard to the window, which said, "More ice."

I asked a nurse passing by if I could talk to this girl, and the nurse said, "...It's incredibly dangerous to go near one of them. Their fire could ignite you, too. We have an intercom set up if you'd like to speak with them."

"Oh, no worries. I'd really just like to talk face to face." I said.

The nurse frowned under her mask to me, and said, "I don't believe I can let you do that. If an outbreak occurs this whole building could be in flames."

"...What if I just got her some ice?" I said.

"...I guess. She always complains about it not being cold enough in her room and always asks for more ice... I'm terrified every time I have to go in there... so just be quick." the nurse said.

The nurse got me a big bag of ice, and unlocked the door for me to visit this girl.

It was even colder than outside. I shivered a bit, but the girl looked rather comfortable.

"Hiya!" I said, "I got you some ice."

I handed the ice to her, and she thanked me. She said, "Oooh. This is the good kind. How did you get them to splurge for me?" and weighed the ice bag in her hand.

"Good kind? Isn't it just frozen water?" I said.

"Yeah, but this brand is from the Yukon. It just tastes better." she said, and opened the bag and started eating the ice.

I sat in the one chair in her room as she sat on the bed. The ice made a crunching sound under her teeth. Crunch, crunch, crunch.

"My name is Yule, and I'd like to ask you a few questions about your condition, if that's ok." I said.

"Serenissima. Or you can just call me Sera. Whadda you wanna know?" Sera said.

"How did it happen to you?" I asked.

She looked deep in thought, and said, "We had a broken fuse. My dad tried to fix it himself… and he did, every few months. We just didn't have the money to pay for a proper electrician or repairs, so my dad jury rigged a bunch of things together. He spent all his time on that fuse box… One day he was too drunk, working on the box, and made a slight mistake. His hand caught fire, and the house was soon ablaze. My mom quickly went down into the basement to help him, to put him out, but she caught fire too. I didn't know what to do… My family was burning alive, the house was filled with smoke… My mom told me to leave the house quickly before she went downstairs with that fire extinguisher, but all I could think about was my pet turtle.

"My dad originally got the turtle so we could have turtle soup, but I thought he was so cute. I fed him lettuce every day, and he was probably my best friend. He didn't say a word, good or bad, but was always comfortable around me and came out of his shell when I picked him up and put him on my lap. I loved that turtle, so I quickly went into my room to go get him.

"My turtle was hiding in his shell, and I picked him up and tried to run downstairs, but the stairs were engulfed in that demonic fire. I screamed, as the smoke filled my lungs. There was no way out besides the windows. Then the fire caught onto my leg.

"I threw the turtle out the window, thinking that at least I'd save him. He landed on the street, and a car ran him over. I looked down at him as I was screaming, as my legs were burning… and I jumped out the window.

"I was on fire, wounded on the ground, and someone put me out. I didn't know who he was, but he wrapped me in wet blankets and took me to the hospital as quickly as he could. He left the turtle dead on the street, but at least I was alive."

"Gosh." I said. "Sounds like you've got a guardian angel."

"The man visited me for a while, just to see if I was alright, but he's too busy nowadays." Sera said.

"Ok. I was shot with a demonic fireball and that's how I got infected." I said.

Sera opened her eyes in surprise, and said, "Really? And you can still walk around… *outside??*"

"Yeah. I've got someone working on my case now. This cold is actually not so bad." I said.

"You still feel cold? I feel kind of lukewarm, honestly." she said, and crunched on another piece of ice.

The nurse was tapping on the window, and I said, "I guess I gotta go. I'll come visit again sometime, if that's ok."

"Sure. Want to see a drawing I made of the man who saved me? I keep it hidden because they usually don't want anything flammable in our rooms." Sera said. She beckoned me over beside her bed, and hidden under a panel in her bed was a folded piece of paper. She unfolded it, smiled, and showed me the picture of the man who saved her.

I gasped, as I noticed the extra incisor in his smile. The man that saved Sera was the same man who tried to kill me.

Zaxazaxar.

21

I frowned as I walked down the street thinking, as Clippers harassed me with pointless info and notifications.

Why did Zaxazaxar hate me so much? So much that he'd even try to kill me?

I sighed. It felt like my clothes were getting too warm, so I went back to Lux.

He was busy at the workbench, but said, "Alright. Here we go... one more twist... and it's all set! These clothes are perfect! It'll be sort of a cast until I can think of something better." and he showed me the metallic breastplate, gauntlets, boots, and legguards on his bench.

They were all black, and frost was accumulating on them. I said to Lux, "Uh... Is that even clothes? It looks like a suit of armor. And... Er... Isn't it a little... spiky?"

"Hm? Isn't that fashionable?" Lux said.

"I guess it does look like something a punk rocker would wear." I said, touching the armor. It stuck to my hand from the pure cold emanating from it, but my hand soon melted off the ice and I rubbed a hand down the black plate.

I put on the armor, and it was freezing, but I did feel safe with it on. I never wanted to feel that hellish burning again.

The gauntlets had spikes on the fist, and I threw a punch in the air, imagining stabbing Zaxazaxar with them.

I thanked Lux again, and he told me to stay cool.

I went to the strip club, to turn in my resignation.

Missus M stared at me for a second in her office, and said, "You become some sort of prude all of a sudden?"

"I really do love working here. I feel happy, for some odd reason, showing myself off and making other people happy. But I can't with my new… condition." I said.

"One of these women doesn't have any real feminine parts on her. What condition do you have that could be worse than that?" Missus M said.

"Tracy? Yeah, I really don't know how she does it. I only noticed when I was changing with her one time. As you can see… I need to remain clothed. Cold clothed. I was burned with demonic electricity." I said.

"Hmm… What if you just became a sort of manager? It would really break my heart to see you go. You keep morale up, and always have time for people, the other girls and clientele." she said.

"Really? I would love that! What do I have to do?" I said.

"Talk to people." Missus M said, and smiled.

I wandered around the strip club, in my black armor, talking to the customers.

I started with a flirty smile, maybe a wink.

Then they'd buy me a drink, and we'd continue the game.

Until I got to the meat of their troubles, their sorrow and pain.

I took them to the back rooms with the beds…

Sat them down…

And let them cry on my shoulder.

Everyone has their own troubles and sorrows. Everyone suffers. And some just need someone to listen to their problems for a while.

"I'm just so sad! I'm just so angry! I just want- I don't want-" a man said as he was bawling his eyes out.

"Shh. It's ok. I'm certain that a better position will open up for you soon. I think it's great that you're still teaching, even though, as you said, the curriculum has been warped from your expectations." I said, holding his hand with my own cold gauntlet.

"Those poor girls... Straight out of middle school, and into the milk factories. And the boys... only a quarter of them will continue their education, the rest will become gangbanger thugs. I'm thinking about shooting my boss. That bastard demon-" he said.

"Please don't. It will get better. Try to work the insides, change it slowly and gradually, and keep hope. Always hold onto that hope. You *can* make a difference." I said.

He sniffled, and wiped off his tears. He smiled, and said, "Thank you, Yule."

It continued with the next person. When the day was done, I continued my other job, my "hobby."

I cut down the demonic principal as he was getting into his car.

I was masked and armored in black, and the only thing he heard before he died was the whirring of my chainsaw.

I was watching TV with Dina and Doug after work. Cass was out buying groceries. We talked about trying to get a job for Cass, as she had become sort of a shut in. "I mean, it's fine if she wants to bang all day and cook for me, but I really think she should try and continue her life." Dina said.

"Do you think she could be a boxer again?" I said.

"Nah. They don't let you in if you've got robo parts. It's a bit unfair, since the current champion has six arms anyway. They're showing the fight today, want to watch it?" Dina said.

"Sure." I said, and Dina flicked through the channels until we saw the boxing show.

The man was super muscular, and I opened my eyes wide as he flexed all six arms.

His opponent was tiny compared to him, but she had demonic tails like a cat o' nine tails.

They bounced gloves off of each other's, and the fight began.

The demon woman was as fast as a whip, and when she whipped her tails at the man, making him bleed, I didn't know how anyone could win against such a force. Whenever the six armed man swung, she would be out of his way like she was never there.

The six armed man swung all six arms at once at the demon woman, about to catch her...

But Cass came inside, went up to the TV, and turned it off.

"Hey!" Dina said, "We were watching that!"

"The demon wins. It's all fixed in the high ranks." Cass said, and went to the kitchen with her groceries.

Dina and I looked at each other, frowning, and we went to the kitchen with Cass.

"Do you miss fighting?" I asked her.

"Kinda. But it was just a waste of time... I mean, I fought my hardest in every fight, I was going to take the championship, even if they threatened me for not following their made up rules. And then some damned religious woman takes me out before I even get a chance. I guess her drive must've been stronger than mine." Cass said.

"You don't regret it, do you?" Dina asked.

"I only regret that I didn't meet her sooner. I can't get her words out of my head... when she prayed with me. I could've quit boxing long ago, if I only knew of this new way." Cass said, "There's a meeting for people who follow Jesus today, if you two would like to join me."

"People still go to church? I'd love to go with you, Cass." I said.

"Uh… I think I'll just stay at home and-" Dina started.

But Cass said, "You need to meet people with other viewpoints, Dina. And then you start doing that thing with your eyes-"

"What thing?" I asked.

"…Nothing." Cass said, "I'll make some food for us and the other followers, and we can head on over." Cass smiled, making lizard bologna sandwiches, and gave us each one to chow down on.

Cass dressed up in black, masked and hooded, and told Dina to wear the same. I wrapped a cloak around me, pulled up my hood, put on my trusty mask, and we went down to the streets in the night, carrying sandwiches.

It was exciting! Other people who follow Jesus too! I felt like I was rebelling a little bit…

We got to a bar, and walked inside. There were hardly any people there, but Cass whispered a passcode to the bartender, "Spiritus Sanctum," and we were let into the basement.

I passed a man I had seen before, as he was leaving up the stairs we were descending, and I grabbed his arm and said, "I thought I told you to leave."

The man I had saved from an execution looked at me grimly, and said, "You also told me Jesus will be watching me forever now. I just don't get this religion… but I try to understand it. I never knew Jesus was such a ruffian…"

"What do you mean?" I asked.

"The whole thing of him whipping and beating up those people in that church when they defiled it. Couldn't he have started a petition or something? He just seems kind of like a bastard." the man said.

"Uhh… I don't know. I suppose he could've done that in a more peaceful way…" I said.

"And the thing with him being his own father... That throws me off the most. I think I'd rather drink at the bar instead of listening to that insane woman preach at me." he said, and went to the bar.

I shrugged, and we went down to the basement.

It was a bit of an odd mass. The priest, a woman who had two mouths right next to each other, kept on accentuating the vengeance of Jesus, and whenever she did the people would always say Amen. The host, the Body of Christ, wasn't bread but actual meat. I ate it cautiously, hoping it wasn't *really* a person.

At least the Blood of Christ was still wine, but what was an odd sermon turned into binge drinking.

We simply sat in silence, and drank endless wine in this bar's basement. I looked at Cass woozily, as I was on my fifth goblet of wine, and she was silently mouthing the Lord's Prayer.

The priest woman gasped, and pointed at Dina.

"There is a heretic amongst us." the priest said with both mouths.

Everyone stepped back from Dina who was simply calmly sipping her wine.

Dina was grinning to herself, but then noticed everyone around her looking at her, and stopped grinning.

"Letttt's get sommmme air..." I said, and tried taking Dina out the door with me.

But two men stepped before us, and the priest continued in her two tongued voice, "This one is defiled with evil. She is a great evil, masquerading as humanity. We must crucify her, as our Lord died for us."

"Whaaaat?!" I slurred, "Stayyyyy back from herrrr! You peeeeople need to be niccce and friendddly! That's what Jeeeeeeesus would want!"

"The time for that has passed. If the demons only see blood, then we will show them it. Our brothers and sisters were *scapegoated and slaughtered* by them. We need to be ever vigilant now, and all evil must be expunged." the priest said.

They were about to grab at Dina, with me standing in front of her and protecting her, but Cass yelled at all of them, saying, "Jesus is in all of us! Shame on you!"

The people stopped approaching us, and looked at Cass.

Cass continued, "Even the ones most in evil's grasp can be shown mercy. Even the sick, the suffering, like the lepers and possessed. Jesus would cure them, instead of kill them. Jesus is not a murderer! Jesus is kind, and nice, and is probably the coolest person ever! He stood up for us! He stood up against every evil we were capable of! You people make me ashamed! Instead of seeing the light in him, you only see the darkness that surrounded him in his tortured life! Stay back from her, or I'm taking my bologna sandwiches and leaving!"

The priest muttered, and said, "Those *are* pretty good smelling sandwiches... What did you put in them?"

Cass smiled, and said, "Love. That's Jesus's secret ingredient."

The people all nodded in agreement, and Cass started handing out her lizard bologna sandwiches. They all sat down and ate the food that Cass seemed to have an unlimited supply of. I calmed down and talked to a few of the flock, and most were hungry, poor, and unable to fend for themselves. Cass, like Jesus, was feeding the hungry in her own way.

When we left, I slowly shook the priest's hand, and she smiled with one mouth, and frowned with the other.

22

Dina went into the bathroom to "look at something" she said, and I talked with Cass in the kitchen. I said she really said a lot of spot on things about Jesus tonight, and Cass smiled and said, "You make me feel like Jesus is right beside me, watching over my shoulder. Looking at me through your eyes. I'm happy we can share these experiences."

I smiled back at her.

Cass went to hug Doug on the couch, who licked her face.

I went to the balcony to smoke, and looked down at the street. What a nice night tonight. It felt so cold.

I went back inside, and when I passed the bathroom, I noticed it was open on a crack. I looked in, and saw Dina staring at herself in the mirror.

"Are you alright, Dina?" I asked.

I opened the door, and looked at her in the mirror.

Her eyes were black.

"I see…" she said.

"D-Dina. How about you have some tea with me? So you can relax?" I said.

She smashed the mirror with her fist.

Cass came running in too, and said, "Oh no… Not again. What you see isn't real, Dina! Let me bandage you up."

Cass wrapped bandages around Dina's bleeding fist as I watched.

"It is real and it is not. It is naught and all." Dina said.

Cass took Dina to bed, and tucked her in. Slowly, very slowly, Dina blinked her black eyes, and shut them.

Cass and I sat on the sofa with Doug, who was sleeping, and I asked Cass, "Is that happening more frequently?"

"Yes. She sees things sometimes, and sometimes her eyes go black. I think she may have some sort of sickness." Cass said.

"Hmm... What does she see?" I said.

"She keeps on saying she sees someone writing a book. She says she's frustrated with him, because she can't go back, can't escape, can't *something*... I don't know how to help her." Cass said.

"*Why won't you finish me!!*' Dina screamed out in bed. I put a hand on Cass's, as she was about to rush to her, and said I would talk to her.

I saw Dina sitting up in bed, trying to rub at her eyes, but the blackness in them wouldn't go out.

"Tell me who you see." I said to Dina, sitting beside her.

"I see him... that brown bearded man... I saw him writing this now, I see someone reading it... and then I see it again, and again, and again..." Dina said.

"Maybe your mysterious man is trying to help you. I too met someone briefly who passed into my dreams and helped me. Maybe you should listen to what he has to say." I said.

"All he cares about is the book... See..." Dina said, and looked into my eyes...

And I couldn't see.

Then I saw someone writing a book, looking down on Dina through words and descriptions.

He didn't notice me at first, busy as he was writing, but he took his eyes from his computer for a second and smiled at me.

I had seen this man before. I think we met in Düsseldorf. He was with a woman named Lucy.

He waved to his books, a book about Lucy, a book about Paul, and a book about me.

He said he has thousands more that need to be written.

"Who are you?" I asked.

"I'm just the author of this book. But even this portrayal of me is just words, a mirror image of a mirror image." he said.

"Isn't that just the original then?" I said.

He shrugged and said, "No one knows what two mirrors portray when shown to only each other. I kinda think they show nothing at all, just like if a book remains unopened, the world inside will never be."

"I think you're kind of pessimistic." I said, "Someone is bound to open that book, someday."

He sighed, and said, "I hope so."

Then he started writing again.

I saw something out of the corner of my eye, and looked outside of the room.

I saw you.

Clippers hopped on my shoulder, and told me I had one million new emails.

I opened my eyes in fright, and Dina was looking at me with normal eyes again.

"That's what I see every time. At first I saw that writer, then I saw… now I see a white rabbit." Dina said.

I looked at Clippers on the bed, and said, "I see the rabbit too."

She waved a hand at the bunny, and said, "Thing is everywhere! I updated my phone, and then it had that bunny on the screen, trying to 'help' me. Now I see it telling me to check out every new porn site on the internet!"

I looked at Clippers, and he was just sitting there.

Dina soon went to sleep, she said whenever she saw things she got very tired, so I let her rest and let Cass take care of her.

I thought to myself as I wandered down the street. I thought either I could go get a drink with Jake... or go get burgers with Lucius...

It was so difficult to decide! I liked both of them!

I just sighed, and even though I tried to tell myself I wasn't, I knew I was having boy troubles.

Damn men! They each were interesting in their own way! I thought it was a bit odd that these two were in my love life... They both scraped with death, in different ways. I wondered what they thought of me?

I called Jake, as Lucius had traded his phone for the flute, and Jake was already drunk, "Heya, Chainsaw Chick. I was just waiting for you. Did I tell you I'm injecting myself with this poison from this exotic jelly-fish? It's a fuckin' rush! I nearly died twice!"

"I seriously don't know why you do that." I said, walking down the street.

"Well... It's not only a penance thing, it's a trial by fire. And of course, if anyone tries to kill me with that stuff, I'll just get back up and kick their arse. You should try it with me sometime." he said.

"I think I'll pass. I'm already infected with demon electricity, I don't want to infect myself with anything else." I said.

"...Oh! So is that why you're all clothed in black metal these days? You mean... you can't take it off?" he said.

"Nope. Lux is working on something else to regulate my body, but whenever I take his pills I get really woozy and can't stand up straight." I said.

"Kinda sucks that a stripper can't show off the goods. And you've got a nice pair of goods! Whatever. Are you coming to the pub or not?" he said.

"...You mean you don't care that I have to remain clothed?" I said.

"I mean… It's a bummer, yeah, that first time we went to bed and you choked the shit out of me… I thought there was something magical. But that's alright. You've got a winning personality." he said.

I smiled, said I'll join him there soon, and hung up.

I was on my way to the pub, but I heard this mystical sound in the evening as I was crossing a bridge. I peeked my head over the side and listened to the sound of the flute music.

I saw Lucius sitting on a rock in the middle of the rushing water, playing. I called out to him, and he nearly dropped his flute into the water, but caught it and fell in himself. He was being rushed down the river, and I jumped off the bridge to save him.

Oh right. I was wearing thick metal plate.

I sunk immediately, and tried to claw my way back to the side. At least the river wasn't pushing me downriver too hard.

I gasped in water as my head resurfaced, and saw Lucius make it to the bank. He scavenged a piece of wire, and threw me a piece of the cord. I grabbed on, and he pulled me back to the bank.

I sputtered up water on my hands and knees, and Lucius helped me up again, holding his flute.

"Thanks, Lucius." I said.

"You really have a ridiculous streak of trying to save me, Yule. I was fine, y'know." he said.

"…I know… I just got worried, is all…" I said.

He was shivering, but we hugged, and he shivered some more under my cold.

"I-I th-think I-I'm going to start a fire, if that's ok." he said, chattering his teeth.

"Fine by me." I said, so we sat by the remnants of a campfire under the bridge, and Lucius started a little fire for us with flint and tinder.

"So that fire inside of you won't go out?" Lucius said.

"Yeah. It's that crappy demon electricity… Stupid stuff." I said.

"At least you don't have to worry about the cold winter. I mean, I've only seen it snow twice in my life, and that black snow is cold as fuck… But it is beautiful." Lucius said.

"It sucks that even the snow is black here." I said.

We just chatted about the weather for a bit, and then I asked him if he could play something for me.

He put the flute to his mouth…

And made a wet muffled sound out of it.

I laughed, and said, "Oh right… Duh."

He smiled, and while I could probably just chat about the weather with him all night next to the crackling fire, I had already told Jake I was going to meet him, so I gave Lucius a cold hug goodbye, and went to the pub to drink myself to death.

Jake and I stumbled away from the pub, and got Dantinis. He actually was starting to enjoy the pork.

We went to a movie, and he tried to put his arm around my shoulder, but quickly stopped as the cold nearly froze his arm off.

I waved him goodbye, on my way back home, and I *knew* I heard… that peaceful, enchanting flute music on the wind.

I went to Lux's, and just stared at the beautiful, albeit fake, tulip picture on the wall.

Damn men!

23

I was smoking a cigarette outside of Lux's home, and watching the moths attack the flickering light on the corner.

I thought I heard that horrible angry scream I had heard before again, coming from the lamp, from the very electricity.

I walked over to it, but the scream was dwindling, dwindling, and soon gone.

I had goosebumps everywhere, and I shivered not from the cold, but from that horrible agonized scream.

I walked back into Lux's home, and he had some good news for me.

"I think I can get you to fly." Lux said.

"Really?? How?" I said.

"Um, I know you *won't* like this… but I can attach some wings to you with a surgical procedure." Lux said.

"…It won't hurt, will it? What kind of wings are they? Not bat wings or somethin', right?" I said.

"No, wings of fire, like a jet's. Although… I tweaked them a little bit, just for your style, and they should look like something heavenly in themselves." Lux said.

"Ok… I guess- I would like to fly up there, to that big black tower… How are you going to do it?" I asked.

"Please, undress and get on the table, face down. I will be applying freezing water every few minutes, and performing transfusions for the blood loss, but you shouldn't have any pain with the gas-" Lux said.

"No. No drugs. I really don't want to pass out and not be able to wake up again... You can perform the surgery on me when I'm awake." I said.

"...Are you sure? I need to attach them to the nerves where your previous wings were." Lux said.

"Yes. Just give me a strip of leather to bite on so I don't bite my tongue off." I said, and got undressed.

I immediately felt so... *hot*. I felt like I was burning as I laid on the table facedown, but Lux immediately applied the freezing water on me, and I felt better. It sure didn't feel freezing to me.

Lux picked up a small, sleek plate of metal from his workbench, and walked back over to me.

He gave me the leather to bite on, and then he picked up the drill.

I started sweating, but I didn't want to lose consciousness again. I saw Clippers staring at me silently from beside me, and I tried to focus on his soothing white rabbit form...

Then Lux started drilling into my back.

I bit into the leather, shut my eyes as the tears started welling... and listened to and felt the drill pierce me.

I soon was in muffled screaming, biting on the leather, but I remained still as Lux worked.

Lux began screwing the metal on and attaching the nerves to it.

And I could *feel* the metal in me.

Lux continued to douse me with freezing water so I wouldn't burn up, but I probably could've doused myself with my own sweat.

It took a long time to attach every nerve, all night actually, and as dawn was showing through the window, Lux said it was finished as he wiped off the blood.

I slowly, hurting all over my body, got up to sitting.

I looked back at my back, with the metal stitched inside of me.

"So... How are these wings? Don't tell me you need to do more surgery." I asked.

"Try opening them." Lux said.

I could feel the plate, and I could feel... something like feathers....

I tried really hard, pushing open the wings... I heard a sort of clinkety sound in my back...

Then my wings burst out of my back.

I looked back at them in awe. They were white, burning light, fire in a concentrated form. There were *six* of them, like a seraph's in Heaven.

Lux said happily, "I figured out how to use your condition as a boon, rather than a disability. You have *energy* constantly through you, and while it may not be angelic, heavenly energy... you have pure heat coursing through you from the demonic fire. These *wings...* concentrate it, and force it out of you into a useful form. You won't even need the cold clothes anymore! We can take off your cast for good, and you'll be able to fly again."

I didn't feel so hot anymore, the only heat in me was radiating out of my wings.

I jumped off the table, into the air, the sound of my wings burning the air.

I whooped in delight as I hovered. I had missed this.

Even though I was exhausted from the surgery, I could not resist taking a trial run with these brand new seraph wings.

I flew up into the sky, even faster than when I only had two wings, rocketing through the sky in fire.

I zipped past the ravens cawing at me.

I sped past a police helicopter, scaring the pilot nearly to death.

I saw a plane flying under the clouds, and I decided to race it.

I was at its speed in the air, and I looked at a demon child stare at me in awe through the window. She looked frightened of me, as all demons should be.

I rocketed past the plane, instantly passing it by, leaving it in my wake.

I screamed in awesome, magnificent joy, shouting my battle cry to the sky! To the Heavens! "Hallelujah! Hallelujah!" I roared.

But I began slowing, and the flames were starting to flicker. I fell a bit, and tried to keep my heat going until I landed.

It kept turning off and on, I was approaching the farmer's market in the main square, and I landed in a safe pile of squid.

I smiled, as everyone looked at me, and I wiped off the squid guts.

I sauntered back to Lux's, and I felt so woozy.

I was soon shuffling, and collapsed in front of Lux's door.

Lux picked me up and brought me inside.

He placed me on the table I had just had a surgery on, and tucked me in with the dog blanket.

I fell asleep to Clippers's sweet song of pointless notifications...

24

Lux and I went to the park.

We stared up at that big black tower.

"So we're in agreement." Lux said, "We need to stop Zaxazaxar. His world only brings more suffering, his demons, his electricity, and his murderous wrath."

"Yeah. Are you sure I can make it up there? The heat in me only lasts so long before I need to recharge." I said.

"I believe you have a good chance. The few days of reserving your heat we've taken is practically making you sweat." Lux said.

I wiped the sweat off of my brow and smiled.

"Be careful, and keep that chainsaw close. It could be incredibly dangerous." Lux said.

I nodded, and stroked the strap of the chainsaw hanging on my back.

"I'll see you soon, Lux. Make some weed cookies for when I get back, cuz we're gonna celebrate." I said.

"Just… Just be careful." Lux said. I shook his strong metal hand, and got ready for takeoff.

I crouched down, burst my burning seraph wings from my back… waited for the wind to shift… and launched into the sky.

I soared straight up, straight to that abyss in the sky, the dark black clouds pushing down on the Earth.

The ravens tried to keep up, and I smiled and waved them goodbye.

Then I plunged into the clouds.

The heat kept the clouds back, burning through them. I could cut through this dense darkness, and after a long while of soaring through pollution, I burst into the pure blue sky.

I felt like I was blazing in brilliance, as I finally saw the sun again. That pure, beautiful shining light. I admired it for a second, feeling the sunlight on me, and then I saw the peak of the black tower up above.

I flew to that peak, but my fire was getting weaker.

I saw the window on the top, and I aimed for that, put one more burst of fire out, and I turned off my weakening fire, launching to it.

I hit the very top, tried to hold on, but was slipping.

I fell a bit, but grabbed onto the windowsill.

I laboriously lifted myself up and into the window.

I got inside, and I looked around this tiny room, filled with machinery, wires, and someone chained, imprisoned, with devices attached to him everywhere, harvesting him for electricity. I blinked for a second at his ugly handsome face, as he stared at me, I looked at his shredded golden wings, and I smelled the awful smell of a demon's brimstone everywhere.

And Satan said, *"Good Morning."*

Then the devices flashed, and Satan screamed that angry awful scream I had heard before.

He was being drained of every bit of electricity in his soul.

I readied my chainsaw to assassinate the Devil. I had wanted to do this since forever. What a perfect job, what a once in a lifetime opportunity.

The chainsaw was roaring, as I grinned, approaching Satan himself, about to get his final justice.

Satan sighed, and said, *"At least let me go back to Hell."*

I stopped, confused, and said, "That *is* what I plan to let you do."

"For how long? I can't even be permanently damned anymore. I just come back here... over and over. I will murder Zaxazaxar endlessly-" he started, but was drained of electricity again, and slumped over.

I turned off the chainsaw, and stared at him quizzically. I said, "So there is never an end to your suffering? You kinda deserve that, actually."

"I had one more sin to get through... One more, as I was trapped in Purgatory. ALL I NEEDED TO DO WAS SAY SORRY TO GOD. What kind of bullshit... I'm not sorry. I did every, fucking, little thing they asked of me in Purgatory... But then they ask the impossible!! I curse Paul! I curse you, Yule! Every mortal, demon, angel, and God can go to Hell! No... They can go to Zaxazaxar's torture tower! Even better." Satan said.

"It's really that bad, huh? You must just hate it..." I said.

"I didn't say that. I actually kind of admire such torturous vengeance. Zaxazaxar really must be quite messed up in the head... but no... what I hate are those stars. Every little twinkling dot... and the moon, staring down at me mockingly... and then the BLAZING SUN. I HATE THAT AWFUL, RISING SUN." Satan said.

"Most prisoners would find that comforting." I said, staring down at him, "How did you even get trapped here?"

Satan grumbled, and said, *"Language can be manipulated in many ways... He wriggled to freedom in our contract, and bound me. But language does not bind me... chains do."*

"Ok. I guess I'll go, then..." I said, looking back out the window. It was an eternally steep drop, and I couldn't raise an ounce of flame in me.

"You're really just going to leave me here?" Satan said.

"I guess? Why not?" I said. There was no other entrance or exit but the window.

"I've been eternally trapped. I am suffering, Yule. Zaxazaxar is tormenting me, for simple wealth."

"I don't believe you." I said.

Satan laughed evilly, and said, *"Why not? Trust your eyes, if you do not believe my words. What do you see?"*

"...I see a demon being tortured. I see the *worst* demon, you, Satan, being tortured. All that Hell you've inflicted on others... and now you are getting your just desserts." I said.

"Show me some sympathy! Show some sympathy for the Devil! Isn't that what they're always saying? You could have the chance to show the most mercy anyone could ever... You could let an eternally tortured soul find peace. I will never leave this tower, for as long as it stands. As long as this tower of Babel remains, I will be trapped. Would you like that if it happened to you? I hope not." Satan said.

"...I don't know. I'm going to sit for a second and think. Is there really no other way out but that window?" I said.

Satan laughed, and said, *"No. And it is just another form of torture for me, with freedom so close, eternally out of reach. Welcome to Zaxazaxar's torture tower."*

I sat down in front of Satan, as he was drained of electricity again.

Satan was soon whispering to me, promising me everything I could want... if I would only break his chains. I frowned at him.

"You've been killing demons... What if I helped with that?" Satan said.

"You'd kill your own minions?" I asked.

"Of course. What do you think they did when I got here? They laughed. I'd do the same, honestly." Satan said, *"Do you want endless pleasure, instead? You wouldn't be the first. C'mon, sweetie... Let's have some fun. Break the chains. We've got nothing else to do."* Satan said.

"I think I'm fine, thanks." I said.

"It must be so lonely... being a fallen angel. I know how that feels. All those people you left in Heaven... So lonely. You and I... We can be friends. Break the chains." Satan said.

"There are more friends to be found." I said.

"What if you just gave me a dance? Turn a little tricks? I could help you on your form..." Satan said.

I crossed my arms, and said, "That's just work. I don't plan on working for you."

"You must get a little satisfaction from it... being lustfully admired. You have such beauty... It would be a shame to keep it locked up in this tower with me, unadmired." he said.

He was drained of electricity again, and I stared down at my chainsaw in my hand, petting Clippers with my other hand.

"You find an imaginary friend?" Satan said, after he was done gasping for breath.

"None of your business." I said.

"You're probably going nuts, killing all those demons... or maybe you're finally going stir crazy." Satan said.

"I think I'll just try to kill you, and see what happens." I said.

"Go for it. Chop off my arms, if you won't break the chains." Satan said.

I stopped, as I was about to do just that, and sat back down again.

"You could jump for it. Fly out the window, little angel. Fall to death." Satan said.

"You're pretty nasty." I said.

He laughed, and said, *"And we have some time to spend with each other. What fun."*

I sighed... I knew what I had to do.

I could rectify my murders, I could show some sort of peace to some-one. I thought- This was certainly a mistake. But… Should I not show mercy? Sympathy? Kindness? Should I not give a tortured soul a chance to change? Shouldn't I be an angel, a true advocate of God? Showing forgiveness to even the Devil himself?

I started up the chainsaw… and said, "Don't move."

Satan put his chains in front of me, and I chopped them in half.

He rubbed his wrists and got up. Then he started kicking the machinery over and over.

Then he lit his dark red flame in his hand, and incinerated it with a flamethrower blast. He cackled, and said, *"And I am free. Come, little angel. Let's go back to Earth."*

Satan approached me. I tried stepping back from him, but one more step and I would fall out the window.

Satan lunged at me.

He picked me up as I was surprised.

And jumped out of the window.

"Falling is the easy part." he said, as I fell in Satan's arms, down, down, down, through the black abyssal clouds… and saw Friendliness approach from beneath us.

We would soon hit the ground. I clung to Satan for a second, then realized what I was doing. He laughed, but held me close as I let go of him.

His feet hit the earth, making a large crater around us.

Satan immediately dropped me to the ground, landing me on my butt, and stretched his arms. *"Man, you're a heavy bitch. Probably feasted on too much manna and lizards."* Satan said.

"So what are you going to do now?" I said.

"Have some fun. I'm going to kill a few demons who've betrayed me. Want to join me?" Satan said.

"...Um. I don't know..." I said.

"It'll be fun! There's this one guy who sells poisoned meat to children... Malphas, my second in command. He could've been ruling this world... but all he does is sell meat." Satan said.

He offered me his hand, and I took it, getting up, and warily followed Satan into the darkness.

I suppose it would be good to stop Malphas...

Satan changed his form into that of a small child, and asked the demon merchant for some meat.

Malphas, smiling, gave Satan as a child a hotdog.

Satan devoured the thing, and said, "So good! Give me another."

Malphas's grin left for a second, but he smiled and gave Satan another hotdog.

Satan soon ate all of Malphas's meat, and Malphas was just looking at him quizzically as I watched from an alleyway.

"So good... *The poison tastes even better than before, Malphas."* Satan said.

Malphas stepped back in shock, and Satan immediately lunged a clawed hand around Malphas's throat.

"You were such a good second... But you'll always be second." Satan said.

"You shouldn't be here! You were supposed to be locked forever-" Malphas said.

"I'm going to send you back to Hell, Malphas. You and every demon, human, and angel... except the one in the shadows over there." Satan said. I walked out of the alley and approached the two, as Satan started strangling Malphas with one hand. Satan asked me if I would like to do the honors, but I shook my head. Satan shrugged, and split his claws through Malphas's throat, leaving him to bleed out in agony.

We continued to walk through the streets, as humans and demons noticed us throughout Satan's rampage, him massacring every demon that stepped before him.

"It's the Devil!" demons would scream, and flee in terror.

"It's the Chainsaw Chick!" humans would scream, and flee in terror.

Satan laughed as people started panicking, screaming, running for their lives.

The police came in, demons, and shakily aimed their guns at Satan and I.

"La-Last chance, Satan! Go back to jail!" Chief Toose the demon cop said.

"Go back to HELL!" Satan yelled, and the demons started shooting at him, but Satan raised his arm, and incinerated every bullet with a blast from his flame. He reached forth the flame again, and it ignited a car the cops were hiding behind, exploding it, then another, and another.

Satan maniacally laughed at the wreckage, and we walked through the streets.

"Ohhh... I've missed that note. Nothing so beautiful as a good scream..." Satan said, as we passed through the burning street, with *everyone* screaming in terror and pain.

"I'm starting to regret this..." I said.

Satan turned back to me, and said, *"Don't worry about it. I'll save a special place for you... later, as the angel that allowed me freedom. We had a nice little date, don't you think? Lunch... conversation... destruction... Have a good day Yule. That's such a nice name... but I think I'll just call you my sweetie pie."*

"I'm not any sort of sweetie to you-" I said.

Satan lunged at me.

And forcefully kissed me. I tried to escape from his embrace, as he lustfully started groping me. I was about to knee him hard in a vital organ, but he let me go and smiled wickedly.

I instantly tried to smite him down with my chainsaw, but I blinked, and he disappeared before me.

I just ran away, trying to wipe off the feeling of Satan's lips on my lips.

25

I got back to Dina's in the night, muttering to myself... I didn't know *what* would've been the right choice, but I had made an action, and now I was stuck with it.

I let myself in, and saw Dina and Cass doing it on the couch.

"I sleep there, you know." I said, as they were moaning.

Dina wiped the sweat off her forehead, and said, "Shit. Just give us five more minutes?"

I shrugged and went to the kitchen. Doug whined at me, and I fed him a dog treat, as Dina and Cass screamed in pleasure.

They went to the kitchen, clothed, but barely, as I tried my hand at cooking. I was never a superb cook, but I think I could make mac and cheese. I just tried to ignore the part about the dairy being human milk.

They sat at the table as I served them the macaroni, and Cass said, "Er... Yule... You don't mind us... doing what we do?"

I smacked on the mac, and said, "You two find love in whatever manner you like. I don't mind."

Cass said, "We both think you're beautiful, you know."

I stared at them smiling at me flirtatiously, and said, "Um. No thanks. It's not that I'm not flattered! I just don't even know how I would- I just don't- I'm not offending you, am I?"

Dina shrugged, and said, "I get it. You're a prude!"

"What? That's not a bad thing!" I said.

"I'm joking, Yule. I love you no matter what." Dina said, "I just don't get you. Most people fuck anyone these days, as long as their deformity isn't too off-putting."

"So people in general are bisexual?" I said.

Dina said, "Yep. Been a long time since I've heard that word. Sure, there are still some prudes who cling to the old ways, like my ex, Vindicta, but people aren't so sexually confined anymore. It's actually a lot easier finding love, when you don't have to worry about what category you fit into."

Cass said, "I dated someone before who had sex with bees."

"What?" I said, "That's even possible?"

Cass shrugged, and said, "Well, they would all sort of swarm around him as he was naked and- But it didn't work out between us, because he wanted to spend 'more time on the bees...' I didn't mind being second in his love life, but I guess there wasn't room for both me and the bees in his heart."

"Huh. Anyway... I just don't want to intrude on you guys' love life..." I said.

"I would think of it more as an addition to our love, rather than an intrusion." Dina said.

"...Um. I think I've got my heart set on someone else, these days! Yeah..." I said.

"Ooooh." Cass said, "Ok. Which one is it? The executioner? The flautist? Or did you find someone new?"

"I really like-" I started.

"She likes me." someone said, poofing behind me.

I was angry as he rubbed my shoulders. I shook off his claws, as the smell of his brimstone enveloped us.

Cass and Dina jumped out of their seats, and Cass said, "Go away, demon."

Satan sat down at the table next to me, and put an arm around my shoulder. I angrily tried to get out of his embrace, but he just held me close.

Satan said, *"Hey, sweetie, what if we got that nice little pad by the main square? It's close to that pork place you like so much."*

"Just- Fuck off!! Go away, go back to Hell, and just leave me alone!!" I said.

"Can't you tell the connection between us? I think God matched us himself." Satan said to Dina and Cass.

Dina said, "I've seen you before. In my dreams, in my trips… You're the Devil, and you are not welcome here."

Satan laughed, and said, *"Just go do some more shrooms, Dina. Maybe you'll get what you want with the next trip... You won't come back to the living world."*

Dina glared at Satan angrily, and said, "I'll be stronger than you, one day."

"Bullshit. You're the epitome of a stoner's dream, a deadhead stripper. You will have no power at all-"

Dina put a hand to her eyes, sighed, and took her hand from her face. And her eyes were black.

Dina stared into the Devil's eyes, and Satan stared back, releasing me from his hold.

I didn't know what the two saw when they looked into each other's eyes… but Satan blinked.

"I know where you live, Satan. And I'm coming to get you." Dina said, and flicked her eyes back to normal.

Cass started praying, "Our Father who art in Heaven…"

Satan said, *"God... Are you starting your noise too? Fuck this crap, I'm leaving. I'll see you at home, sweetie."*

Satan leaned in to kiss me. I pushed him away, and he laughed, disappearing in smoke.

I just sat there frustrated, as Dina lit some incense to ward off the lingering stink of Satan.

"So... You're dating the Devil..." Dina said.

"What?! No! I just wanted- I didn't want- I'm not dating him!!" I said.

"He seems to think you're dating." Dina said.

"Grr... I should've left him there... and just jumped out the window..." I said.

"Why exactly is that demon following you?" Cass said.

"I wanted to stop Zaxazaxar! I didn't know he had defeated Satan himself! I thought he was torturing puppies or some shit in that torture tower! And now- *I'm the villain! I was always the villain! I am the Chainsaw Chick!"* I said.

Cass opened her eyes wide, and started shuddering, but Dina held my hand, and said, "You're not a villain. You may be *something...* But when I look into your eyes, I see bright light, not darkness."

"So you really believe what you see is sort of real?" I asked.

She blinked her eyes black for a second, and said, "Once you look, you can't unsee."

"Stop it." Cass said, "You know you freak me out when you do that." and then she turned to me, "And you. I don't want to see you around here anymore, Yule. All those people... All killed... by you. You must be a truly tortured soul."

"I only killed demons who were hurting people! I thought I was doing good!" I said.

"I don't know if I can believe you..." Cass said, "Why would people lie about something so horrible?"

The lights flickered off, and there was a blackout. The first one I've ever seen in Friendliness. Doug was watching TV, but started barking at the blackness.

Dina lit some candles, and said, "They want to get a reaction out of people. They want to keep us scared and alone. They want to divide us, to not trust even our friends."

Cass looked at Dina, unsure, the candlelight on her face, and said, "I just don't know…"

Doug scampered into the room, and barked at us.

Dina said, "Shush, Doug. You can't watch your programs now."

Doug whined, and went up to me licking my hand.

"Why does Doug even like you?" Cass said, "Is it because you're as murderous as he was?"

I grumbled and said, "You'd know all about being murderous… Why don't you beat up some more gangsters to be polite?" and pet Doug.

Cass slammed her hands on the table, looking frustrated, and said, "You've been the nicest person I've ever met. You saved me in that dumpster. But why? How do I know you're not going to massacre me and Dina in our sleep?"

I sneered at her, and said, "You guys sleep? I thought all you did was fuck continuously."

"You're impossible!!" Cass said, and got up, walked through the door, and slammed it shut. We heard Dina's car start up in the driveway, and Cass took off.

"You shouldn't purposefully piss off my girlfriend." Dina said, "She's the most innocent, most pure, boxer I've ever met… but she's got a nasty streak that she tries to cover up."

"Yeah, yeah… I know… I used to be like her, thinking everything was so nice… but we live in a rat infested hell…" I said.

"It was never perfect, even in your times. At least we can see evil as it is, not hiding in the dark of men and women's hearts… It is right on the surface." Dina said.

"And once you dig past it, there is only more evil, and more evil, rotted to the core. The only good place you'll ever find is when you die and go to Heaven." I said, crossing my arms.

"Well… What if we went somewhere else for a while? We can have… a little trip…" Dina said.

I asked her what she meant, as she held my hand… looked deep into my eyes…

And her eyes went black.

And I couldn't see.

26

I was singing in the pure, green woods, "Lalalaalalaa..." and skipping with a basket full of biscottis for my grandma.

I put my red hood up as it started raining in the forest.

Ah! The nice rain. It has been so hot these last few days. Felt almost like I had been burned to a crisp...

Someone snarled at me on the path to my grandma's.

"Little Red Raven... walking alone... Little Red Raven... without a home... Come to me, come to me... I want to eat your bonesss..." the voice said.

I gasped, and admired the huge wolf by the trail.

"Howdy!" I said, "Who are you?"

" I'm the Huge Hungry Wolf. Those cookies smell good. Mind if I have a taste?" the wolf said.

"I'm Little Red Raven! And they're actually biscottis." I said, "Sorry, they're for my grandma."

"Hmm... You know what goes good with a gift of cookies? Some nice flowers. Why don't you pick those beautiful black ones over there?" the wolf said, pointing to some black flowers deeper in the forest.

"Hmm... But those are all black!" I said.

"So? Don't you know that's just the way of things?" he said.

"No… I think I shouldn't tarry, and should get to my grandma's, anyway." I said, "See ya!" and waved to the wolf.

"But- But-" he stuttered, but I just whistled and continued down the trail. *"Wait a second, Red Raven!"* he said, and ran after me, *"You've gotta give me time to get there before you!"*

"Huh? Nah… Why would you want to see my grandma, anyway?" I said.

"Listen… I know a shortcut… just through those bushes… If you go that way you should get to your grandma's in no time at all…" the wolf said, putting a paw on my shoulder.

"Oh no! I know this is the fastest route. They wouldn't have made this trail if it wasn't the fastest! See ya!" I said, and skipped down the trail, humming a song about angels.

"But- But-" he stuttered, and ran after me, *"What if we just got time to know each other? Had a little fun? It's not often I get to meet a nice little girl like you."*

"Sorry! I really have to go, and the rain is starting to become a downpour! See ya!" I said, as the Huge Wolf grumbled behind me and I walked briskly to my grandma's.

I got to a nice cabin in the woods, made of biscottis as my grandma made it. I knocked on her door and Mrs. Nestor opened up, smiling to me. She waved me inside and I gave her the biscottis.

"Ahh… Perfect building material. These'll patch up the hole in the roof nicely." my grandma said.

But the door slammed open, and the Huge Hungry Wolf panted, catching his breath, and said, *"What if you-"*

"Hello, Huge Hungry Wolf! Would you care for some tea?" I said, as me and my grandma were drinking tea.

"Um… I really would prefer just to eat you." the wolf said.

"Come now..." my grandma said, "Be a good dog and settle by the fire, and I'll give you a treat."

"Er... Ok. What kind of treat?" wolf said.

"One little pig. The other two are for me and Red Raven." my grandma said, and got us all some pork from her pantry.

We snacked on the roast pigs. Dang! This was some great pork. We all ate the three little pigs happily.

"Well, it looks like the rain is stopping. I've got to go to work. See ya, Grandma! Goodbye, Huge Wolf!" I said, and hugged them each good-bye, and left the biscotti cabin.

I chopped down trees in the forest with my chainsaw. I loved my job, being a lumberjack. Rip, rip, rip... and the trees all fall down!

But someone was watching me work. The handsome man whose chainsaw I now owned. I gasped, looking at his handsome face, at his beautiful body... a body that was now dead.

He said, as he walked up to me, "Please don't leave."

And I remembered the demons in the world.

Everywhere.

I looked at the fallen trees I had cut down, and I saw thousands of demonic bodies instead, cut down by me.

27

I opened my eyes, as Dina looked at me, her eyes pure again.

"What *was* that?" I said.

"Just a dream. Do you want to go back?" she asked.

"I- I- It was nice... but..." I said.

"Real life always has a way of peeking through the cracks. You cannot dream forever, but if you truly feel pain and suffering, if you truly hate this life, you can stay there." Dina said.

"I... I shouldn't leave, not yet. I should stay here... even if there is evil, hatred, and suffering in this world... I should do my best to try and fix that, instead of make it worse." I said.

"And your boyfriend?" Dina said.

I grumbled, and said, "I'll figure out something to do about *him...* But I'd really just like to hang out with the men I prefer, instead of that asshole."

I called Jake, and asked him if he'd like to get a drink. He said he was a little busy.

Huh. He always had time for me, no matter what he was doing.

I went down the streets to look for Lucius, passing his usual haunts, but he wasn't around anywhere.

Where had he gone?

I went to a bar alone, somewhere new, and drank alone. Everyone looked at me, but was too frightened of the chainsaw on my back. I looked around at all of them, wondering what I had done.

The power flickered out again, and someone screamed.

I burst my wings to make light, and I gasped in terror.

Everyone was dead.

A smear of blood was shaped in a heart for me on the wall.

I ran out the door, as looters started breaking into shops and mobs were assembling.

The blackouts weren't doing anyone any good, and I could smell some sort of... *stink* following me.

I turned back, and saw the Devil stalking me, his claws smeared in blood.

I tried to run, but he chased me.

I got down to the river, by the bridge, turned a corner, blinked, and the Devil was before me, wearing a suit.

He said, *"Marry me, sweetie."* and got down on one knee, offering me a ring.

"St-Stay away from me." I said.

The Devil cackled, and said, *"C'mon. What if I was a little more your taste?"*

He changed his form to that of Lucius's.

"I love you, Yule. I've always loved you, ever since I saw you in that club." he said, "You give me a reason to live. We can see those flowers together, forever. We can find beauty and magic in this world, and I- *Pffft... HAHAHAHA!! What stupid sap. You really like the good guys that much?? He's pathetic, a simple bum. You should've let him jump off that ledge... No... You should've pushed him!"*

I angrily walked away, and walked over the bridge.

I was about to walk into the pub, but Satan was inside and opened the door for me. I carefully walked in, looking around for Jake.

The Devil put an arm around my waist, and changed into Jake.

"No one can mess with me, babe. I'm the baddest badass in town, and no one will mess with you, either. I don't care tha' you're the Chainsaw Chick, and actually find that attractive. I jus' love you, babe. You're so passionate, and we make magic in the bed- *HAHAHAHA!! You didn't even fuck him! You could've had the bad boy right then! Is that really what you want? To be some murdering thug's bimbo? You must just want to 'change' him. From what?? A pathetic, sad, murdering monster into your honeymuffin? What idiocy!*" he said.

I ran out the doors and ran down the street.

I was soon crying, thinking of Jake and Lucius.

I heard that flute music haunting me in the streets. It was getting louder, a painful, enchanting, enheartened melody.

Lucius came out of an alley in the distance. He continued his flute music as thousands of rats followed him down the street. I ran up to him, and said, "Lucius!! I was so worried! What are you doing?"

"I'm taking back the streets." Lucius said.

The rats calmly watched him, as he played for them, marching behind him.

There was a man about to stab someone screaming and running through the streets, she tripped and the man was about to catch her and murder her, but Lucius played a note, and the rats swarmed the man, dragging him down into an alley as he screamed instead.

Lucius helped the woman up. She thanked him, and then noticed all the rats. She looked terrified for a second, but calmed at Lucius's music.

Lucius just continued the melody, and the rats, and the woman, followed.

I watched him, as he scared mobs away, stopped murderers and rapists stalking the streets in this now permanent blackout. Lost, scared children and people who didn't know what to do followed Lucius and his song through the city, following behind the rats who once were the menace stalking Friendliness. They called him the Dark Piper.

He seemed not to notice me, as he saved the lost.

I saw a man with an executioner's axe by an ambulance. I shouted out to him, and ran to him.

"Jake!! I was so worried! What are you doing?" I said.

Jake said, "I needed to help someone. I've been working all day for the hospital. I know how to end a life, and so now I am going to help save them instead. I can't talk right now, they need someone to carry people out of this buildin'. We have no electricity, so things are a bit primitive, but I'm doing all I can."

The medics rushed in the building, and I asked Jake, "...What's the axe for, then?"

"Some people get trapped in areas, and they need someone strong to break the barriers. I am needed now." he said, and rushed into the building as people called out to him. They called him a hero.

He carried a woman down the stairs in his arms, and placed her in the ambulance. He seemed not to notice me, as he saved the injured.

Both of my men were busy, and seemed to not pay me the least amount of attention as they took up their callings.

But someone else noticed me.

Satan put an arm around my shoulder, as both of my men passed into the distance, Jake getting in the ambulance and driving off, and Lucius marching through the streets with his army.

"It sucks being alone, don't it. Let's go get some grub." Satan said.

I was soon crying while eating the pizza in the abandoned Italian restaurant... with the Devil watching me devour slice after slice.

"That's what you get for not choosing sooner, sweetie. They'll all leave you in the end... You need to claim them at the start, force them to be yours right away, or they'll find something, or someone, else." Satan said.

I sniffled, and got up, looking at the reviews of the restaurant on the wall.

I saw my old review of this place, framed, now dusty and cracked. Poor lost little Yule Tidings... Everything was so perfect then... even if it wasn't. I had a husband, I had friends... Now I've got nothing.

Everything changes... Even Friendliness had a different name and used to just be a small town, my home... Now it was a blacked out hell, with the Devil watching me crying.

I moaned in agony, and Satan came up to me, whispering sweetly, *"It'll be alright, sweetie. It'll be alright... You've always got me."*

I just cried and cried, as he wrapped his arms around me, and then started licking my ear. He caressed my side, feeling the curve of my waist, and then forcefully kissed me. I just cried and cried, as he jammed his tongue down my throat.

I thought maybe I should accept my fate. I was the Devil's toy. At least... At least... the feeling of contact with him was something...

But I had flashes of a great, albeit short, man as I closed my eyes and let the Devil have his way with me, kissing me roughly and groping my breasts.

I felt like Max, my husband, was directly behind Satan, about to rip him apart.

But Max was dead.

There was only me, and my choices, my actions, my responsibility.

I forced the Devil away from me.

"C'mon, sweetie. I want to fuck you." Satan said.

I burst forth my burning seraph wings of fire, and said, "Leave. Me. Alone. Don't come near me, or I'll finish what I should've done. Go back to HELL. GO AWAY. Do not come back. I will never love you, and all I did was show you sympathy… because I felt sorry for you. You are the most cursed soul in existence, and you should be pitied for that reason. But only pitied, never loved."

Satan stopped grinning for a second, and said, *"So be it. I am the greatest love you could ever have, I am God's first and finest. I should be God instead, and that time will come someday. But so be it."*

The Devil snapped his fingers, and disappeared in a cloud of smoke.

I looked back at the review by Yule Tidings. I certainly had changed. But I was still me.

28

When I got back to Lux, in peace even though it was anarchy everywhere, his home was lit up with electricity, a bright beacon in this hell.

"You still have electricity?" I said inside.

"Oh, I never use demon electricity. I use the olden methods... compressed dinosaur bones. I always preferred having something that wouldn't cut out on me in case the world goes back to Hell. "

He offered me weed cookies on a plate, but I said I wasn't in the mood.

"Something wrong? I knew as soon as the power went out you must've stopped Zaxazaxar." Lux said.

"I- I- I don't know. Everything is awful outside, and people are terrified." I said.

"Hmm... Why don't... you talk to a few of your past enemies. We, with them, could bring about order again."

"Who exactly?"

"The vicious crime lords you have mercilessly stopped. Vindicta, Amare, and even Daemonia. I mean, heck, they bring more law into this city than even the cops do. We all live in a rigorous code of laws enforced by each other."

"We?" I said.

Lux said, "I am Lux, Latin for Light. You don't get a Latin name in these parts for just existing. We are the underbelly of society. I, Lux, fill the world with light, as you can see by my home, and I, Lux, will bring light in the darkness of the streets. Now is the time to change everything. I always expected you to have power... even though you do not have electricity. Now, my experiment can truly take off... We, together, will change this horrible Hell, as you have defeated its overlords, Zaxazaxar and his pet minion, Satan-"

"You knew he was harvesting the Devil?? And you still let me go up there??"

"Er, yes. But don't fear! Now that Satan is dead the world will truly be safe-"

"Um... I actually let him go."

"You did *what??* I thought you hated demons!!"

"I do... but... I just didn't think it was right to kill him, or leave him chained up there."

"Hmph. I do not understand you. Every step of the way you throw off the experiment. First, I just needed you to make electricity, but you cannot, then, I wanted to see if you could exterminate every demon, but quite frankly that would take forever and you got blasted by Zaxazaxar anyway, now I want to truly raise the stakes, and in my hand I am holding nothing!!"

"Hey. I am not nothing. And have you ever stopped to think that the golem that brought me to life was really brought to life by me? You were aimlessly making and selling drugs before. Now you're talking about saving the city. I think you owe me. You've changed, Lux. Despite your nonexistent soul, you've changed against your will."

"...I don't think so. I'm just reacting to certain stimuli in the appropriate manner and-"

"I don't know what will happen to you when you die. But, by your identity, your *soul,* you've become the Lux you are now."

He grumbled, and said, "Fine. You win. I'm a new being. Happy?"

I smiled, and said, "I think so. Let's go talk to our past enemies. Shall we?"

"Let's go, Yule." Lux said.

We walked out the door, and Lux led me to the first gangster's hideout, Amare's.

We knocked on the door of this trashy mansion, and Amare himself opened the door, smoking a cigar, bandage where his extra arm had been, as he was naked to the wind.

He immediately got a little aroused when he noticed us. I thought he was getting stiff because of me, and was a little peeved... but then I noticed his eyes never left Lux's crystalline eye.

"You've reconsidered. Come in, come in!" Amare said, grinning and waving us in with one of the arms he still had.

His huge pet lizards hissed at us, and Lux said, "Um, no, Amare... I still think we should remain separate, but we need your help reclaiming this city."

We sat on the sofas, I with Lux on one and Amare on the other, Amare sitting wide open with his dong pointing to the ceiling. I tried to ignore it.

"Really. I don't know, we've already got numerous places under our protection, and things are really looking up for the gang. This constant blackout is going to make us rich. I can... finally get that comfortable waterbed... Lux..." Amare said.

Lux said, "Well, if you cannot see reason, we will go talk to the other gangsters and-"

I said, "Lux wants to go on a date with you."

Lux and Amare both looked surprised. Amare said, "...Are you sure? After all this time... I just thought you were playing hard to get, Lux, but then it seemed like it would never be. What changed your mind?"

I nudged, Lux, and Lux said, "Um. Your big, hairy penis."

Amare broke out in a happy smile, and said, "Really?? What do you like best about it?? I do adore compliments on my body… Go on! What do you want to do with it?? Be descriptive!"

Lux said, "I just want- I want to-"

I said, "It's a very nice penis, Amare. You must be proud. But you should save it for your date. It will be a magical night, I assure you."

Amare grinned, and said, "Of course, of course… Don't want to wear myself out before the fun even begins! Well, I'll see what we can do for you. We can lead squads to bring the lesser thugs to justice, appropriate food and supplies from the rich, and then hand them out to the people who are in hard times. My! This has been a wonderful little meeting. Please, stop by again sometime." and he shook my hand, and then Lux's, and whispered to Lux seductively, "And Lux… wear something nice. I do love seeing you walk around naked all the time… but just wear maybe a short skirt and top? Something pink…"

Lux sighed, and said ok, and we left the mansion.

I laughed my ass off, as Lux walked embarrassed beside me.

We went to the hangout place of Vindicta's next, but all the thugs said Vindicta was just drinking hooch and smoking meth these days, in a stupor in his trailer. We went to the trailer by a trainyard, and knocked on Vindicta's door.

He opened up, scratched at his neck, and said with drowsy, hungover eyes, "Whaddaya want… Can't you see I'm busy?"

"Hi, Vindicta. We need your help gathering the gangs to put order back into Friendliness-" I said.

"It's *you*. I'll kill you, and then I'll find that robo bitch!!" Vindicta said, and tried grabbing at my neck with his seven fingered hands.

Lux pushed him away, and said, "Vindicta, you are probably pretty pissed at Yule and Cass for putting you in your place, but there are greater matters to concern yourself with than petty vengeance."

Vindicta huffed, and said, "I don't care what happens to Friendliness. There are demons hunting people, randomly stalking the streets. Let them eat everyone, not like I give a shit. I'm just going to smoke another bowl."

"...Demons are on the rampage?" I said.

"They don't even *act* like people anymore. They're just fucking monsters running around. The children ones... they give me goosebumps. Nothing scarier than a child singing some demonic song and dragging someone's severed, bleeding head through the streets..." Vindicta said, and started a cigarette.

"...We need to do something about that. I'll go on the hunt immediately and cut them all down-" I said.

Lux said, "No, Yule. You cannot kill every demon in Friendliness. We need you, Vindicta. We need your people, your weapons, and your... skill." Lux said.

"My skill? Everyone says I lost! That stupid robo bitch- No one fucking respects me anymore... Next time, I'm just going to shoot her in the head, instead of risking my reputation on some stupid fight. That bitch will get her comeuppance soon, I swear..." Vindicta said.

Lux said, "This is actually the perfect way to reclaim your reputation. When you massacre even monsters from Hell... who could ever say you lost? They would not only praise you as a true huntsman, they would call you a savior as well."

Vindicta rubbed his goateed chin for a second, and said, "I would like to show those bitches who doubt me their place... but... I want to fight that robo bitch again..."

I said, "I'm not going to let you shoot Cass in the head."

Vindicta frowned, and said, "Well aren't you smart. Vengeance isn't served fair... It's served when your enemies are all dead, and you're laughing at their corpses. I'll be coming for her someday..."

I said, "Let it go, Vindicta. You're not making any friends."

"Fuck friends. I'm gonna go skin some demons, and then we'll see who needs friends. All I need is *Vindicta...* and some of my guys. It's no fun showing off to yourself." Vindicta said.

Lux said, "I'm sure you'll find endless praise when the demons lie dead. Think about it... who needs to kill a cyborg who hasn't even killed one demon? Let her live, and you can show her her true place."

"Huh. Never thought of it like that. Why is she a cyborg, anyway?" Vindicta said, "She get some sort of nasty rash?"

I said, "Demons cut off her arms and legs because she followed Jesus."

Vindicta frowned, and said, "That's fucked up. Man... I'd be so angry if someone took my arms and legs..."

I smiled, and said, "Yeah. She is."

Vindicta said, "Ok. Well... I suppose I can show her how real men take care of those who've wronged them. That'll show her... Yeah..." Vindicta looked down, and continued, "I've lost so many people to demons. They don't look like normal citizens when they're ripping your guys apart and eating their entrails. I'll get some vengeance... for Friendliness."

He then went back inside, and brought back out a tommy gun. He slammed the door, and charged off to gather his crew.

Lux and I were then following Clippers, as I asked him to take me to Daemonia. The internet was disabled thanks to no one having electricity... but I knew where she would be, watching a show that I was sure she would keep alive...

We got to an apartment complex, abandoned, and walked up the long stairs.

It was spooky in here, and the halls were all vacant of life.

We looked around, following Clippers, and soon were at the top floor. I heard a heart monitor beep out... that someone was still alive here.

We got to the door at the end of the hall, and I creaked it open.

I saw the eternally dying demon woman in the bed. She raised her eyebrows at me, and looked frightened.

There was a man with no ears sitting in a chair in the corner, with a laptop pointed at the demon woman.

"This is your end, you know. This is your final justice, Darcy." the woman in the computer said. The man with no ears turned the computer to us, and Daemonia said from on screen, "Hello, Lux, my dear man. Chainsaw Chick, great work on stopping Zaxazaxar. I assume you want your payment now?"

"No…" I said, "We just need your help with the other gangs. We need to reclaim Friendliness."

She started laughing, and said, "This is exactly what I wanted. I wanted this city to burn in fire… It will only be so long, before demons are hunted like they should be, before the rich become peasants again, and *I*… will rule this world. Or just… enjoy the show."

I looked back at the dying demon woman. She was trembling.

"You'd really just sit back and enjoy the destruction? That's quite heartless." I said.

"Do you think I have a heart? I am digital, the most destructive virus on the internet, and moreso, a copy of a demon. And you made all this possible, Chainsaw Chick." Daemonia said.

"…And I want to make it better again. Will you help me do so?" I said.

She sighed, and said, "I am eternally backed up on the internet. I will always be around… someday. This is only a brief rest for me, as someone finds me again, and I take over again, and again, and again… This change means nothing to me. Why *would* I help you to draw out my eternity? I'll win eventually, either way."

Lux said, "You can change. I know what it's like to feel… so heartless, but you can change, as you can change the world. You can be admired and loved, instead of feared."

"Lux… You once tried to love me. We had such deep conversations, and I truly saw something 'lovable' in you, as you did in me… But you and I, we don't need to care." she said.

Lux said, "But- But I do! I have- friends now. I have people that I can care for. Who needs pleasure when you can find happiness in other ways? I can find happiness in other people, and I think you can too."

"I just want to watch the show… If you truly care for me, if you want to be… my *friend…* I will give my assets to you. In this lifetime. You can owe me with interest in a couple thousand years. Money is worthless right now, but my company has lots of stored products that you and your gangs could find useful." she said.

"Thank you, Daemonia." I said, "We won't betray your act of generosity and friendship."

She giggled, and said, "It's so easy to go into business with a friend… They can be *taken advantage of.* So. End this show, and I will watch yours."

I looked at the demon woman attached to tubes and wires. I sighed. I decided I would give her mercy.

I would end this poor woman's life. This tortured, evil soul… I would give her peace.

For otherwise the virus would continue watching her, letting her suffer in misery.

I went up to the plug, and pulled the cord.

Darcy the succubus blinked for a second, and slowly… shut her eyes.

29

Lux and I got the gangs properly equipped with Daemonia's assets. We were practically military with riot gear, flamethrowers, even a few tanks, and many other weapons and supplies.

The demon cops shot anyone they felt like. I saw one pull someone over in their car, give them a ticket, and then shoot them in the head. The cops sped away, laughing, as I tried to catch them with my chainsaw.

But our thugs, who were all humans, kept the cops quite busy.

Vindicta had hit squads of people rampaging through the streets, rushing demons with bayonets, obliterating them with grenades... and the demons were not happy.

The demons *devoured* people, they used any weapons they could get their hands on, but they were all extremely deadly even just with their claws, fangs, horns, and tail. We lost a lot of good criminals in those alleys, as Amare and his thugs tried to save people.

Any hooligan causing chaos who was a human was quickly put straight by his gang... or else. They then went on to rob the rich, some rich snobs who were either privileged demons or humans who bowed down to the demons' reign, and made them just a little bit more like the rest of us. Their mansions were safe zones for people now, and their hoards of food kept the hungry from starving.

While we were resting in one of these safe zones, Amare stared at the beef, and said, "What... *is* it?"

"That's cow flesh, Amare." I said.

"I've only seen pictures of cows. They breathe fire from their snouts and shit gold, right?" he said.

"Hardly. They're rather peaceful creatures, with no golden anuses." I said.

Vindicta had just come back to the mansion, sweating and covered in blood. But smiling.

"See! See, guys? Told you I could take on that demon by pistol whipping him to death." Vindicta said.

People admired Vindicta, respected him, even loved him. He was putting all his efforts into slaying monsters. Little did they know it was for such selfish goals, but still, even selfish goals can cause good sometimes. In his breaks, he told stories of the many demons he killed, all true his gang of thugs said, and let the women stroke his legs, arms, and chest on the sofa.

Lux came out of the back... in a pink skirt and top. Amare dropped his jaw in awe at Lux, saying, "You are the most beautiful woman I have ever seen." I just tried to keep from laughing too much.

Dina was petting Doug, sadly looking at him as he whined at her. "I don't know where she is, boy." she said.

Dina's apartment was attacked, she wouldn't say if they were humans or demons, since she just called them psychopaths, and she and Doug had fought for their lives. She blew them apart with her shotgun, and Doug tore out their throats. Cass was still missing.

I went out to the back, and found Lucius playing for his new gathering of followers. They spoke of him like he was a mythical legend, like a fairy tale come to life, and I guess he sort of was. His rats guarded the perimeter, unseen, but still there. Jake stood by the side and watched Lucius play, Jake's axe by his side, and I stood beside Jake.

Jake was enthralled by the music. He was rocking his head gently back and forth to the music, and when it was over he applauded with the rest.

He turned to me, happiness in his three eyes, and said, "I never knew it felt so good… helping people. I thought I was doin' good *before*… executionin'… I just feel ashamed of it now."

"We can all change. I'm glad… that you feel bad! That's what I wanted from you since the beginning." I said, smiling.

He smiled, and held my hand… but all I could think about… was Max.

I let go gently, smiled, and said, "I just need to be alone for a while."

He nodded sadly, and said, "I understand. You like 'im." and waved to Lucius, "I get it. Chicks love music… Well, I've got an idea…"

He went up to Lucius. By the way he was walking it looked like he wanted to fight him or something… but Jake just asked Lucius to teach him how to play the flute.

Lucius opened his eyes wide, and said, "So how did it work out with Yule? Did you ask her yet?"

"Er, she kinda said no before I could. But that's cuz she likes your stupid awesome music!" Jake said.

Lucius said to me, "Hey, Yule, wanna go out?"

I smiled and blushed, as Jake grabbed Lucius by the collar and said, "You bastard… You're not supposed to just blatantly blurt the question! You gotta lead up to it with somethin'!"

I went up to them, as Lucius was grinning and Jake was threatening to punch him, and said, "I really do like you both… and it is a very difficult choice. I don't want to lead one or the other on, so I'm just going to remind myself of the love I had, and think on that. Maybe one day in the future… but not right now."

They both frowned. "Kinda disappointin'." Jake said.

"Yeah…" Lucius said.

"But I know! How about we start a band! I know how to play harp, actually." I said.

They both looked at me quizzically, and Jake said, "I guess we could make some sort of folk band."

Lucius said, "Yeah, that'd be alright. As soon as things go back to normal, or whatever will be normal, again."

I smiled, and kissed each of them on the cheek.

30

Dina, Doug and I were searching through the streets for Cass. We knew she had to be somewhere... on foot too, as we found Dina's car crashed on the side of the road. Thankfully there was no blood in or around the car, so we figured Cass was at least alive.

We searched everywhere for her! We were silent, however, not risking to call our her name... because otherwise the demons would get us.

They slithered and lurked around every dark shadow, waiting for us, watching us. Now that their time was about to be over, they fought all the harder to prolong it.

The sound of them growling at us got a little unnerving however... and soon we ran inside the old church, looking for some shelter from the demons in the night.

Dina locked the doors, and we breathed out a sigh of relief. Doug started sniffing around... and then barking happily. He ran through the church, where we found a woman with robotic arms and legs praying to where the cross would be if the demons hadn't torn it down.

But she wasn't praying alone.

She was praying beside a man who looked like someone who looked exactly like Paul, the Spawn of Sax.

They turned to us, and Cass said, "Oh. It's you two. Hello. Meet my new *friend,* Zaxazaxar."

"I see you survived." the man she was praying with, Zaxazaxar, said to me.

I burst out my seraph wings of fire, and stared at him in hatred.

"Wait... I know that voice..." Dina said, thinking hard for a second, then gasped, "YOU'RE SPAWN OF SAX!! Holy Hell!! I knew you were alive, I knew it!"

Zaxazaxar smiled with that extra incisor smile, and said, "Not Spawn of Sax, I'm afraid. More like spawn of spawn of spawn of spawn of... You get the idea. I'm glad people still listen to and enjoy his music after I put it on the radio."

Doug sniffed at Zaxazaxar for a second, and Zaxazaxar put a hand out for Doug... which Doug shook with his paw.

"How did you get him to do that?" Dina said, "He's never, *ever* done that."

"Just animal magnetism, I guess." Zaxazaxar said, and then waved his hand and Doug rolled over for him and allowed Zaxazaxar to rub his belly.

"Stay away from him, Cass. Get over here, quickly." I said, wielding my chainsaw.

"No, *Chainsaw Chick*. Zaxazaxar believes in Jesus too. Zax was actually doing good in the world, keeping Satan imprisoned... You let Satan free." Cass said.

Zaxazaxar said, "I suppose it couldn't have lasted forever... despite all my best efforts. I was sure the Devil would kill you."

"Just like you tried to?" I said.

"What does she mean, Zax?" Cass said.

Zaxazaxar stopped rubbing Doug's belly, and lit a cigarette in this church, lighting it with his *demonic flame* coming from the machine on his wrist.

"I tried to kill the woman who nearly ended my ancestors. Maggie and Paul... they were both there, in that church that this woman did *nothing* in. I tried to kill the woman who was mercilessly killing other citizens... for some sort of vengeful, sadistic purpose." Zaxazaxar said, smoking his cigarette.

"I see... Then she really is a murderous monster..." Cass said.

"What?! Don't listen to him! Paul and I fought the Devil together!" I said.

"And now you've let the Devil free. It is not the other demons' fault that they were brought to creation by greedy and foolish people. It is not their fault they ended up on a hellish Earth instead of Hell. I tried to live peacefully with them, creating a utopia where every damned soul can find peace. I defeated the Devil, I subjugated the demons... but you ruined it all, Yule." Zaxazaxar said.

"You're just trying to toy with us. I don't believe a word of your good intentions. You only created a utopia for yourself. It *is* Hell out there! IT ALWAYS WAS! Ever since I came back to life, this place has been the worst, darkest, horrible pit of a city! And you are basically its king. You are the King of Hell, Zaxazaxar." I said.

Zaxazaxar grew furious with me, and said, *"Do not speak to me so. Your kind abandoned us!! Your God brought us suffering, ever since he threw us out of the garden...* You are the villain, angel."

Cass said, "Z-Zax... Try to calm down. I'm sure you can rebuild-"

"No, dear Cassidy. It is over. The time of humanity will never be. God will rule us all, with an iron thumb... or the Devil will destroy us in fire. We could've overthrown them both, with our wits, our intellect, our technology... But that will never be." Zaxazaxar said.

Cass said, "But God loves you. I'm sure he does, and would never force us to serve him. We just have to watch out for people like the Devil."

"But I do not love God. I only admire his so-called son. I do not respect a God who allows people to cause such *evil...* I do not love a God who allows hate to roam rampant." Zaxazaxar said.

"Please." Cass said, "Try to listen to what God is trying to tell you. Just listen for a second."

Zaxazaxar sighed, but listened to the silence with Cass, as Dina and I were quiet.

Zaxazaxar said, "...I hear nothing."

"Exactly." Cass said, "God lets you have peace, silence, and calm. He allows you to think for yourself, to act on your own choices. We all make mistakes, Zax, and God allows us the power to make them. It is because he loves us, and cares for us, and would never do something to harm us, even if we are harming ourselves."

"I've heard enough silence." Zaxazaxar said, and lit his flame from the machine on his wrist, "I have nothing left. I will at least end my line with our enemies ended as well."

"No! Please don't!" Cass said, as Zaxazaxar shot fire at me.

I launched to the ceiling of this church, Zaxazaxar shooting fire at me, launching a flamethrower of demon electricity at me. I bounced from wall to wall, zipping around the demon electricity, dodging nimbly and gracefully, swerving through any opening of flame I could find.

Cass tried to grab at his arm, but he pushed her to the ground.

I launched at Zaxazaxar, with my chainsaw soon at his throat.

"If I start it you will be gone." I said.

"Do it, Yule." Zaxazaxar said, "Do your final evil. Carry out your foul God's will, and allow me eternal damnation."

I was about to, remembering the pain he inflicted on me, but it was his face. It was so much like a face I loved and cared for, exactly like Paul's... besides his angry grimace with that extra tooth.

"Your soul has a chance at redemption." I said.

"I don't believe I have a soul. Therefore I don't. You will end me *permanently*. And that is a better fate than either Heaven or Hell." he said.

Dina came up to us, as Zaxazaxar and I were both angrily glaring at each other, me pinning his wrist down and my chainsaw at his throat. Dina said, "Shh. It will be ok, Zaxazaxar, Yule… It will be ok…"

And we looked at her, and her eyes turned black. She grinned to herself…

And we couldn't see.

31

I laughed with Zax. My husband had died, and me and Zax... We just really got along so well. We actually met at the graveyard, as he was also in mourning for his wife.

We reminisced about our previous loves, and we comforted each other as well.

We went out for drinks, and he had the most unique, charming opinions on God! "I find Jesus to be more of a role model." he said, "It really doesn't matter if he's real or not, he is a good example of what we should be like. All those possessed maniacs, prostitutes, and lepers he hung out with... Healing and protecting them. Even though I think his story is far too, er, *miraculous...* I try to live up to the story."

"I love going to church. It's the community for me. Wherever you go, you can always relate to another Christian. Even just a story can bring people together and create good." I said.

We smiled to each other, and I took him home with me.

I showed him my pet rabbit, Clippers, and Zax said he was the cutest bunny alive. Clippers just looked so comfortable in his arms...

We drank coffee and watched TV for a bit. We were hardly watching the show, and preferred our deep conversation on the couch.

Then before we knew it, we were kissing each other, laughing in delight and happiness on the couch.

He kissed me softly, as he undid my bra.

I felt his manhood, and enjoyed his excitement.

I was on top of him at one point, he was on top of me…

We screamed out in pleasure as we climaxed.

Then we just relaxed on the sofa, laying in each other's arms. What a fantastic evening.

Then Dina walked in the room, and said, "See. Even someone you hate could be your best friend, if you allow them to be so."

Her writer tapped out the words, "Good point, Dina. Should we allow them to continue this fantasy?"

"Nah." Dina said, "They already live in one that is much more exciting. Let's let them wake up."

"If you say so." the writer said.

Clippers buzzed an alarm, and I woke up, still laying next to Zaxazaxar… but in the church, with my chainsaw in my hand, and Dina staring down at me and grinning, and Cass staring down in fright.

Zax- I mean, Zaxazaxar, blinked open his eyes, and said, "What… What did you do to me? You rooted out the memory of my wife… and replaced my love for her with *her*…"

"I don't like you doing that to me anymore, Dina." I said.

"Oh, no worries… You're very welcome for showing you both a good time. I'm thinking about selling this gift, but eh, I will never get past the end, anyway. I'll just go back and say, 'Yeah, thanks for watching my pitbull when I've got those extra hours for my side job.' and you know what happens next…"

"I… I don't understand…" Zaxazaxar said.

"I think she's trying to tell us she's psychic or something." I said, getting up. I slowly offered a hand to Zaxazaxar, and helped him up.

"Um… Was that a real… experience we had, Yule? Did you mean what you said when we talked?" Zaxazaxar said.

"I think so. I... uh... think we should maybe try to stop killing each other, if we both feel that's ok." I said.

"I think that would be... ok. I won't say I want to go back there... but I'm just not sure what to do with this life, in my 'pit of a city' as you put it..." Zaxazaxar said.

"Let's talk to our crew of thugs and criminals, and see what we can do. You're not a bad person, Zax. I think you've just made a few mistakes." I said.

Zax said, "And I don't believe you had any part to play in my ancestor's death... I just- am so confused... and I very much miss... Rita... my wife..."

We walked out of the church, and I asked him what happened to her. Cass and Dina were holding hands ahead of us, as Doug led the way.

"She died giving childbirth." Zax said, "We would've named him Paul... If only I hadn't made a stupid deal with the Devil..."

"What did he promise you?" I asked.

"He promised me that my wife would be able to get pregnant. I would've done anything to have a child with the woman I loved, to continue my line with her... but of course, it was just a cruel joke, as my wife and my son were both taken from me. But I found an error in his demonic contract... The same way he could take my soul, I could take his. I summoned him again, one last time, prepared, and I caught him, I captured his soul, and locked him on Earth. I improved Sasha 'Sinful' Sally's work to an epitome of greatness... It even landed me in jail a few times, as I tested my work on the demons that were already summoned to Earth and landed positions of power. I eventually finally escaped... and showed the demons I was not to be trifled with by imprisoning their master, and stealing Satan's soul with our knowledge." Zax said, "This device on my wrist was actually the key to the Devil's binds. There is none other like it, so I was wondering how you released him."

"Huh? I just used my chainsaw." I said.

"...That cannot be right. The chains were impervious, and this key, lock, and chains were made from a piece of the Devil's soul..." Zax said.

"I thought you didn't believe in souls?" I said.

"I... I didn't, which is why I foolishly accepted a contract with what I thought to be an immortal monster." Zax said.

"Can you even steal the Devil's soul? What could you do with something so warped and twisted? Wouldn't he just do the same thing you tried to do? Just say he doesn't have a soul?" I asked.

Zax said, "...I never thought of that."

"I'd take that thing off, if I was you, and not mess with creatures like Satan ever again." I said.

Zax looked down at the device on his wrist, like a manacle.

He tried to undo the machine, but it stayed locked tight.

We heard horrible, menacing, awful laughter in the wind.

We hurried down the street, as the Devil laughed at us.

The others were a little wary of Zax, but Zax tried his hardest to smooth over any ruffled feathers.

Vindicta stared Zax in the eyes with a cold stare, and said, "So it's the big chump himself. What are they always calling you? The famous scientist/entrepreneur? You must got a lot of bitches in that tower of yours... Big ol' demon bitches with big ol' titties, from all that energy you were harvesting..."

"Um, no." Zax said, "I only had my research equipment there. I lived down on State Street."

"OHHHH... So the big chump only had his research equipment... It's a shame you aren't in your tower, big guy... *Cuz I'm about to blow your head off.*" Vindicta said, and jammed his pistol into Zax's eye.

I tried to tell Vindicta to leave him alone, but Zax just said, "I get it. You think I've been living in a gilded cage and leaving you all to rot. My home only had two stories."

"I live in a trailer, chump." Vindicta said, jamming the pistol harder into Zax's eye.

Zax was raising his demon electricity handcuff up to burn Vindicta, but I quickly went to him and lowered his hand. I said to Vindicta, "You won't get any street cred for killing some chump, Vindicta. He's not worth a single bullet."

Vindicta holstered his pistol, and said, "Got that right. Go outside with the ratboy, chump."

We heard a flute make a sharp sound, letting Vindicta know Lucius heard, and Vindicta jumped.

He quickly said, "I mean go outside and listen to the Dark Piper's tune. It's really something magical..." and walked away, shaking his head.

Zax and I walked outside, and listened to Lucius play his tune. The people never seemed to get tired of it, and always said it made them feel safe.

But Jake came out back too, with a giant guitar, an axe.

"Ok... Listen to this, guys." Jake said, and strummed the guitar. He tried singing some song, but his voice cracked and he couldn't really hold a single note.

A child was putting her hands over her ears, but Jake ignored all the people's disgruntled faces and tried singing with his guitar anyway.

Zax said, "...Are you trying to cover Spawn of Sax?"

"I *am* coverin' Spawn of Sax. Quit your mouthing and listen." and Jake played a guitar solo. Some of the people were getting up and walking away.

"Here. I know all the words. I think you were just making things up for every other verse." Zax said.

"What?? I know the whole fuckin' thing!" Jake said.

"Play 'Kasey's Dishwasher' then." Zax said.

Jake grumbled, and played guitar, and right as he was about to sing a note, Zax jumped in and sang instead.

"You've got a broken machine, clanking like sin...

Rattling back and forth, and about to blow off the hinge...

But you're a man, and you've got a plan...

You're gonna fix that damn thing,

You're gonna smash it to pieces, and put it back together again!"

The people were astounded by his beautiful voice. The people leaving came back, and listened to Jake play guitar and Zax sing.

Lucius smiled, and played his flute with the two.

I sat down and smiled, listening to the music.

I saw Lux walking with Amare down the road… Lux in his pink skirt and top and holding hands with Amare.

I grinned, and walked over to them, as the band played.

I listened to their porch side conversation as I was hidden behind a bush. Lux said, "Um. It truly was a rather nice evening… I never knew you could do things like that! And I know all the tricks in the book!"

Amare said, "Comes with a passionate heart. You're a truly nice girl, Lux, but I think we should take it slow from now on… You're just… Whenever I look into that crystal… I just get too horny. I got jobs to do now, I've gotta keep people safe, and I gotta keep a cool head."

"Sounds fine, Amare. It was an enlightening experience." Lux said.

Then the two kissed goodnight, and Amare went to his car, waving Lux goodbye.

Lux stared down the road as Amare left, and kept staring even as the car was well out of view.

I coughed, and said, "So you two had a nice night, I take it?" and came out of the bushes and went beside Lux.

Lux was extremely embarrassed, and tried looking away from my grinning.

He tore off the skirt, threw off the top, and said, "I only put up with it. Just an act, to get him on our side."

"Oooh sounds like someone is in denial! C'mon… Tell me how he pleased you!" I said, as my grin widened.

"I cannot feel pleasure, so he didn't please me in the least." Lux said, crossing his arms and looking away.

"C'mon… Please? There shouldn't be any secret between us 'girls,' right?" I said.

Lux just ignored me and walked inside.

I laughed my ass off, sighed out after a good laugh, and looked up at those dark clouds.

I could get past them, if I desired, but it would still be nicer to see the setting sun on the earth.

I took a short walk around the block. Those corpses were still there... but not for long, as the ravens and the rats devoured the pieces of flesh left on the bones. The ravens cawed at me. I looked up at the power lines and the line was completely populated by ravens. They stared down at me silently.

I sang for the ravens in German, my native language, singing a song I had learned as a kid from my tribe.

I burst my seraph wings, and flew slowly into the air, as I sang and the ravens flew around me like a tornado.

I finished my song, dropped gently back to the earth, and bowed to the ravens who flew away again. Someone clapped softly, and I turned to the man who was watching.

Zax said, "You've got a beautiful voice."

I smiled at him, with his eyes opened in awe. I said, "I was actually trained by St. Cecilia in music, so I better!"

He looked up at those black clouds, and said to me, "Was it always so dark in the world?"

"There was always evil... but at least everything didn't look so black." I said.

"I've never seen the actual sun before. Rita always would draw it in different ways, imagining what it would look like." Zax said.

"Want to go up there with me? I can show you." I said.

"I'm sorry... but no. I think I would've preferred to see it with Rita. Thank you for the offer though." he said.

I smiled sadly, and said, "I understand. I miss my husband, too. He had the best sense of humor, and was the bravest man I've ever met."

"To be as bold as to marry an angel... I imagine he must not have been afraid of anything, even the wrath of God." Zax said.

"Hardly! It took all his courage just to ask me out! But he wasn't brave because he was fearless... He was brave because he overcame his fears." I said.

` Zax nodded, and said, "I became sort of numb after Rita's death. I felt no emotion, not even fear. I had lost my heart, and without its constant beating, life became meaningless. The only thing that kept me going was thinking about... about my enemies, like I thought you were. I imagined everyone who wronged others, and villainized them in my head. It didn't matter if they were demon, angel, or some other lost sheep, their sins weighed heavy in my mind, but instead of doing what Jesus would've done, forgive them, I damned them. And now... I carry each and every sin, sins of my own and others. Is there any way... to make it not so heavy? Will I need to sacrifice myself as Jesus did?"

"No, I believe not, Zax. Forgiveness starts at home, so try and forgive yourself first." I said.

"Ok... Should I do what that executioner does and slice myself? Or maybe I should just end myself by jumping off a building, as I believe forgiveness to be an impossible task..." he said, looking down at his feet.

"Jake actually hasn't killed anyone lately, so just has those scars to remind him of his sins. He will carry those scars forever, and even though they say you can't change a tiger's stripes... I think he doesn't need to add any more of them.

"Lucius once felt like you, thinking that the world would always be dark and evil, and unable to live with it and himself, he nearly committed suicide. But the littlest things have ways of bringing happiness and peace to us... like a gentle melody, or maybe just the dream of seeing flowers.

"You just need to take it one day at a time, try to distract yourself from evil and darkness with the light and goodness of the world. You may make mistakes in life, but no sin is truly unforgivable to God, if you learn from that sin and try to change from it."

"I suppose…" Zax said.

"Good. It's getting darker out, so let's get inside before some demon jumps us." I said.

We hurried inside, as the darkness over the sky loomed overhead.

33

We were slowly taking back the city! Demons were fleeing Friendliness, as more and more of our people took up arms and saved the rest.

We all cheered when we got the TV working, because we harvested any bit of coal, oil, wind, and water in Friendliness under Lux's guidance, and used power sources besides demon electricity.

We passed around the beer, and drank and laughed. We were going to have a little party!

The TV was just blatant static, but we kept it on to remind ourselves that things were going to be normal again. Doug still watched it, if anything.

Dina and I danced the tango together, as everyone watched. At the end, I leaned her down and kissed her as everyone cheered. She was blushing, and coughed. Cass giggled.

I just relaxed on the sofa with an arm over each of my two best friends, Dina and Cass. They both had their hands on my thighs, one hand with an arm full of tattoos, and the other a cyborg's strong metal.

I admired a painting, a beautiful, intricately designed piece of artwork. This mansion had so much stuff in it from its previous occupant, who used to be some *very, very* rich demon. She was the fattest demon I ever saw, and it's a good thing she's dead now. She killed at least five people with that huge mouth of hers, with all the many, many teeth.

At least she had a good taste in food, and we had stores and stores of provisions in this place. I took my eyes off the painting as Dina and Cass started making out right in front of my face, and admired them instead.

I enjoyed it very much.

They stopped kissing, giggled, and looked at the three men with gaping mouths watching us three. Dina and Cass waved to Zax, Lucius, and Jake.

Dina and Cass got up, and I slapped both of their butts, then went over to the three men. I said to them, "Well! Let's play some music!"

They all stuttered and nodded.

I started on the huge harp, playing a gentle melody. Plucking a string here and there, and people quieted down to listen to me play.

People sighed in contentment, as I washed away their sorrows, their pain, their suffering, with just a few notes.

The people all clapped for me when I was finished, and I bowed to the crowd.

Then Lux started a beat on the drums. He was hardly any different than a drum machine, and kept the tempo exactly precise.

Jake played the guitar, very drunkenly, but still with this sort of wild energy that was hard to match. His axe, his constant companion, was now a different sort of axe, but still making heads rock and roll.

Lucius played the flute, loudly, defiantly, and with the most grace I had ever heard. It was hard to resist his tune for some reason, as he pulled at your body with only a flute. It was a mysterious, haunting melody that left you wanting more.

Zax sang, in a voice that everyone swore that they had heard before... Just like Paul's, the singer of Spawn of Sax.

I picked up the bass, and kept us all connected, kept us in tune... pulling my heartstrings for my band.

We rocked all night! People were dancing, getting drunk, and partying. This was probably the most fun I had ever had in Friendliness.

But Doug started barking over the music, howling, and Dina and Cass went to him. He howled in a sort of painful way, but stared only at the static on TV.

Dina said, "Shh! Everyone, quiet down. Something's happening."

We stopped playing in the middle of our song. I went up beside Doug, trying to calm him down. But he just stared at the TV.

Then the TV wasn't static anymore.

A man on screen coughed horribly, and said, "Listen, everyone. I have something important to tell you.

"This broadcast is from the other cities across the country... We have had constant blackouts for a while now, and everything was hellish... As you probably are also experiencing, the demons are no longer nice and cuddly. They're killing anyone they can, torturing them, and bringing horrible suffering on Earth.

"And Satan walks amongst them.

"But we are fighting back strong... We've nearly taken over this whole state again, and things were on the right track.

"But the disease, the one that we have to wear masks for... Is on the rise. No, not on the rise... It's an epidemic again.

"I needed to warn you..." and he started coughing some more, "to leave. Find somewhere else to hide. Do not trust other people's very breath and-" cough, "remember to pray. Everyone in this state has the sickness, and I too will die soon. There is no cure. Please. Pray for us."

Then the TV was static again.

Everyone was eerily silent.

Then Clippers was on the screen. He simply asked us if we would like to open our emails.

34

I honestly expected demons to cause the world's end, not some natural disease.

I sighed, as we loaded the stuff into the van. Jake, Lucius, Zax, Cass, Dina, Lux, Doug and I were going to traverse the country, maybe go to South America for a while, or maybe up to Canada. We hadn't decided yet, but we knew we wanted to leave Friendliness.

We stopped by the strip club before we left Friendliness, and said goodbye to Missus M.

Dina hugged her in the strip club. The place was empty, and Missus M was about to close it down for good.

Missus M said, "Goodbye… granddaughter."

"I'm gonna miss your crotchety face, Grandma. You take care of her, ok, Tom?" Dina said. Tom nodded beside Missus M.

I also hugged Missus M, saying, "Thank you for giving me a place in the world."

She sighed, and said, "Don't worry about it. You made me rich, practically. I can afford Tom as a permanent bodyguard and caretaker now. We're going to go somewhere in the tropics, somewhere nice. I'm going to miss my cat… but it's probably best to leave him here with someone."

"Your cat?" I said, "Please! Can we have him?"

"Hm? As long as you feed him well. He likes fresh fish, but I'd give him a tiny piece of steak just to spoil him every now and then." Missus M said, then went in the back and brought out a cat carrier.

I gasped at this cat.

Besides the new fat rolls, he was exactly as I had seen him before in my other lives.

He mewled up at me.

I opened the cat carrier, and picked him up, petting him in my arms as he purred.

I put him in the van, and whispered to him, "You *are* Rasputin, aren't you?"

He smirked at me.

I giggled, and we started off to our next destination.

We went to the memorial we built for all the people's lives who were taken by demons. I looked at all the many graves and monuments... and I placed my chainsaw on a very certain grave. Even his gravestone looked handsome, in a way. We said our respects, Cass, Zax and I said a few prayers, and then we continued onwards.

We were on our way out of the city as Jake and Lucius were arguing about what to name our band.

"We can't be the Dark Piper's Rats! I ain't no rat! And you're not the main star, Yule is!" Jake said.

"Well we're certainly not being Tiger Stripes. It sounds cliché... and it's just a reference to that messed up thing you did!" Lucius said.

Zax said, "Spawn of Zax?"

They both shook their heads at him.

Cass was looking at a map in front, as Dina was driving, and Cass said, "I think it's the next exit..."

"Ok, but last time you said that we went around in circles." Dina said.

Lux was looking out the window and sighing. I was sitting beside him, and said, "What's wrong, big guy?"

"I destroyed all my research. Every bit of soul electricity... is now gone. It feels like I worked all that time just for nothing..." Lux said.

"Why did you do that?" I asked.

"SSS's work brought horrible consequences. I could not bear to see that again, in a different form. I made you suffer, Yule, by giving you life... and I am sorry." Lux said.

"I think you also unwittingly caused some good as well. But yes, the afterlife should remain after life, and not cross in between." I said.

But Lux still sighed, and said, "And Amare never called me again..."

I said, "You know he has a lot to do. He and Vindicta are practically the government in Friendliness. I noticed that new notch on your arm, though... and I'm sure he feels the same way."

Lux looked at the heart notch on his arm, which said in the middle, "Amare Amor."

Lux covered the notch with his hand, and said, "I hope so."

We looked back, and by the side of the road I saw the billboard which said, "Welcome to Friendliness!" as we were leaving it.

We stopped to camp in a campsite in a tiny park, one which actually had trees. We put up our tents, and got inside as it started to thunderstorm.

I yawned awake in the morning and went outside of the tent. The rain had stopped, and the sun was shining brilliantly... It felt like a good, normal day in the forest.

I gasped.

The sun was shining.

I looked up at the clouds, and there was a brief crack in that covering of abyssal clouds.

The crack seemed to grow wider, as I told everyone to come outside and see this.

They gasped at the sunlight, at the pure blue sky in that crack of clouds.

Zax knelt, and said a prayer for Rita, as he was bawling his eyes out.

We all watched that sunlight for a long time, feeling very happy.

We continued driving down the road, as the light of the sun shone down on us.

Epilogue

Instead of going to Heaven, Hell, or Purgatory, I watched over Yule, as she gently accepted that I was now dead.

I was still a lost soul in limbo, purposeless and aimless besides my one purpose to guard and guide Yule, but as I watched her drive down the road, someone found me and offered me a job, someone who was accustomed to death and suffering…

God. Because he knows what you are feeling too, and is always there for you, even at the very end, even if you've committed horrible mistakes, or are in awful, unimaginable suffering.

I asked God, "Shouldn't you send my soul to eternal damnation forever insead, to feel the pain and death I inflicted on Yule?"

He just offered me a better position, and said I was a very shrewd negotiator. He said I would get one hundred percent job satisfaction, I would get eternal hours with complete tenure, and I would even get a company car.

I asked him, "…What do I have to do?"

He said I had to help others through the same pain and death that Yule and I had experienced.

I became an angel of death under God, driving my pale car to help the suffering and dying, a comforting hand for them as they breathe out their final breath, bringing their souls to Heaven in a gentle drive through the clouds.

I do wish the car wasn't the *same exact one* that I had killed Yule in…

But I was happy my new boss had a sense of humor, and I worked forever, paying off my debts to the God I owed everything to.

I was still a guardian angel on the side for the angel of war I loved, but Yule had finally found the light, and as I helped others through death, she would continue her life.

www.ingramcontent.com/pod-product-compliance
Lightning Source LLC
Chambersburg PA
CBHW070352200726
48294CB00003B/868